De...

Sean Burke

Library of Congress Catalog Card Number: 2002105202

A complete catalogue record for this book can be
obtained from the British Library on request

The right of Sean Burke to be identified as the
author of this work has been asserted by him in
accordance with the Copyright, Designs and Patents
Act 1988

First published in 2002 by Serpent's Tail,
4 Blackstock Mews, London N4 2BT
website: *www.serpentstail.com*

Typeset in 10.5 on 12.5pt Ehrhardt by Intype London Ltd
Printed by Mackays of Chatham plc
10 9 8 7 6 5 4 3 2 1

This novel is dedicated to Patricia Waugh and to John Williams

Deadwater: still water: eddy water closing in behind a ship's stern

Pharisee [M.E. *pharise*, fr. O.E. *farise*, fr L.L. *pharisaeus*, fr. Gk. *pharisaios*, fr. Aram *pĕrīshayyā*, pl. of *pĕrīshā*, lit. separated; akin to Heb *pārūsh* – separated, distinct]

BUTETOWN, 1989: SPRING

'Why do you look for the living among the dead?' Luke

Chapter One

Everything is in front of me, she thought as the train windows blacked out. I can't get rid of it.

She wouldn't ever know that it was the Severn Tunnel that decided her, nor that Bristol Parkway was the furthest from Wales that her short life would take her. She got off mid-journey with no more of a plan than the intuition that put her on the Paddington train in the first place.

At Parkway she chain-smoked, dragging so heavily on each cigarette that she felt queasy. When the announcement of a train came over the intercom she had no sense of how long she'd been looking at the late-afternoon sun on the wet, tingling tracks. She didn't listen, didn't look at the computer screens or the posters on the carriage windows. She simply boarded the train because it looked like the one she'd boarded from Cardiff.

'Where are you going?' the ticket inspector asked.

'Cardiff.' Two harshdirt syllables, spat out as though it hurt her to say them, like a sailor's last Capstan-grained cusses.

'Sorry,' the ticket inspector said. 'I don't understand. Your ticket is one-way from Cardiff to Paddington. You're travelling backwards.'

'I changed my mind at Bristol, all right?' she says, making a point of flicking her ash into the aisle. 'I gets on the train and thinks I don't want to go to London. So here I am going back to Cardiff.'

She's conscious of people trying not to look at her: somehow her fear is so great that it's started to faze the world around her. She feels like she hasn't got a name, a history, a place to come from or to go to, scarcely even a face: just that black leather jacket, defensive downcast eyes, auburn frizzes and off-blue stonewashed jeans.

The station guard looks her up and down. Younger than the hardness in her eyes, the sneer about her lips: twenty or so, he estimates. Black leather jacket, blue jeans, a kind of Afro perm. On a white girl that has to be trouble. He wouldn't see the vulnerability behind the little toughie act.

'Your ticket's not valid. I'll have to take your name and address.'

'Christina. But my friends, they calls me Tina.'

The inspector regards it as one insolence too many. She realises that there might be a pathetic little hassle if she doesn't play the game. She gives her official address.

'Christina Villers, 28a Loudoun Square.'

'That's in the docks in Cardiff.'

'Butetown is what it's called.'

'It's all the same thing down there,' he says. Her address has confirmed his impression of her as low-life scum. She knows, retorts with her own look of special contempt.

The ticket inspector lets it go, eyes raised as if offering up his small mercy for notice.

She could only feel safe where she was in danger: Butetown. You could only play the gangs off against the coppers for so long. Whoever got to her first would show her a way out.

That was the hope; that was the dread.

The Butetown skyline looks ugly as the train slows into Cardiff Station. All leading towards the docks and the deathly cold room of custom. It was like she was being sucked back into something. Why had she come back? Christ, she'd only fucking left two hours ago and thinking she was gone for good. But what the fuck was London to her? She didn't know anyone there. The only plan she had was the £500 she'd conned from the Baja brothers in a roundabout way. Better to confront her fears, she thought now. Better to use the money to buy her way out than land up lonelier than she could imagine in London.

The sky was grey and full of something as the taxi took her the short ride to Argyll Square. She must get some good money tonight. She'd started hustling there three years ago before moving on to the Butetown pitches. It was as safe and secure a pitch as she'd ever found; just around the corner from her Auntie Babs's house, her father drinking in the nearby cluster of pubs. A couple of miles from Butetown and its docks, gloomy and heavy now, when it had been easy money and endless parties a few years ago and where, for tonight, she must resign herself to the most dismal of beds. Hustling in Argyll Square and sneaking back to Butetown to sleep – it was more than she could stand. Perhaps tomorrow she'd call in on Auntie Babs: but her old man had found she was on the game and there'd be all fucking hell to pay, most like.

'Christina,' she says in another carriage. 'But my friends, they calls me Tina. That do you? That all right?' she asks, exhaling from yet another cigarette with brisk and brash defensiveness. Lanky guy at the wheel of the small, beat-up car: looked like a friendless student. Another one of those limp-dick weirdos and a task before her harder than coaxing dawn fire from dead coals.

'What's your last name?'

'Why you putting this heaviness on me? There isn't no fucking names in this, you know. That should suit you; and it certainly suits me.' She holds his gaze.

'What's your fucking story anyway?' she whispers, as much to herself or the air as to him.

'Sorry, it's all a bit impersonal.'

'That's the whole fucking point, isn't it?'

'It just makes me nervous, that's all.' Unused notes fluttering in his pocket, like the butterflies of a stomach on being called to this event. A car without headlights screeches from a side street.

'There's an accident looking for somewhere to happen,' he says, turning towards her.

Cut the friendship thing, creep, she thinks. I don't need this: not now.

He said he was cold and miserable and wanted to smoke a cigarette first. She kicked off her shoes, pulled a condom from her handbag, waited.

'Whenever you're ready,' she said absently, but with a hint of mewling, of low moan: a once-full voice falling away from itself like ash from a cigarette or wood-shaving from a lathe.

She leaned to the passenger window, unbuckled the belt of her jeans. She liked to keep her black leather jacket on unless they insisted on going at her nipples. Somehow the jacket made her feel cool, safe, in control. As if she feared for herself from the hips up.

Two or three more punters, a short taxi ride to the docks and it'd be tomorrow. Then she'd think her way out of this. She was still just – but only just – OK with the cops. But if she testified then she'd blow it with them and the other hustlers to boot. If she didn't then the Bajas were after her. She wasn't wanting any of it any more. Her Auntie Babs said to get off the drugs first, but she wouldn't understand, sweetheart though she was. How could you hustle if you didn't do a few drugs? And how could you buy the drugs if you didn't hustle? It's not that simple. You just got by one day at a time. And waited for something to change. So one morning you'd be settled and you'd have a baby and all this would be just bad memories.

But she knew it wouldn't ever be like that. That's what she'd dreamed of with Tony Baja and look where it'd got her. She could see her father poncing a pint off her with his told-you-so attitude. 'Why don't you find a nice white man, Tina? White man, white woman: it's natural that way.' She'd heard that shit all the way through her teens. And what had happened with Tony Baja was nothing to do with black or white. It was to do with drugs and fuck-ups. 'There's black blood in our family,' she'd reminded her father: with which he takes a swing at her; catches her, a real beauty.

'Youth's on your side, love,' Auntie Babs had told her. 'And you'll never know how beautiful you are. Some decent man will love you, love you enough not to mind what you've been in the past.' No man will ever love me, she'd said. She knew that. The streets were her only security, and she was in all sorts of jeopardy there.

Just before midnight, another car flashes its lights at her. The wrong type of car, but she could handle it. She gets into the back seat.

'Heard you were living above the bookies on Angelina Street,' says the copper in the passenger seat.

'This little room I uses for business. It's not mine. I don't live there.'

Two weeks ago and I wouldn't be lying, she thinks: the chilly room Lida lent her with a mattress and a three-bar electric fire. The room of business that now doubled as a hide-out.

As he waits for a radio response, the copper asks her to empty the contents of her handbag. A speed-dusted make-up mirror, a couple of passport-size photographs, two department store cards, lipstick, a powder compact, three loose but unopened condoms, a half-exhausted pack of Berkeley cigarettes, a book of matches carefully folded into its lip.

The main copper fingers the make-up mirror, tastes the sulphate. 'Not the best in the world, is it?'

'Is what?'

'All right, love,' he says. 'Just keep off the main street. And anything you hear about those Baja brothers, you know . . .'

She walks back to Argyll Square, looks up, down and around. Rich, healing tears well up in her eyes. She cuts a small line of sulphate on her mirror. She remembers a couple of cans of Breaker in her holdall, opens one, takes a good gulp.

Rainy now and Easter Saturday and no late licences in the city centre: a profitless night, she suspects.

Chapter Two

The first thing Jack Farissey registered was a steady throbbing between his index and middle fingers. Opening his eyes he saw the curtain of coloured plastic strips that somehow reminded him of the saloon bars in Westerns. Then he saw rows of soft-porn mags wrapped in cellophane, realised he was in the back room of Sven Books. Next, he saw Jimmy the Hat sitting in a hard chair. Hatless, Jimmy yanked a clump of tousled, salt-and-pepper hair from his head. He put the clump into his mouth and began chewing.

'Shh,' Jimmy the Hat said, passing him a bottle in the half-light.

Farissey swigged on the bottle without looking at the label or colour. Vodka, he supposed, from the sharp, spartan taste. The insides of his index and middle fingers had blistered into soft, translucent domes. He separated the fingers and scraped the charred butt of a Park Drive cigarette from the flesh.

'Tut-tut,' Jimmy the Hat grinned. Hairs protruded from between his teeth. 'Tipped fags are better for you.' He looked elfin without his headgear. 'You only pose as an old boy, anyway.

Wake Jess up,' Jimmy the Hat said. 'I'm ringing the Big Man by appointment. He'll take you somewhere to get cleaned up.'

Farissey clambered to his knees. It took five or six shakes to get a response from Jess Simmonds as he lay, head back, in the leonine mass of his blond hair. His shirt was unbuttoned, revealing the taut, muscular mass of his chest along with some blood in its light, almost colourless hairs. Just as Jess murmured 'what?', Farissey noticed the heavy smudges of blood on Jess's yellow shirt. Farissey looked down at his own clothes. His dark crombie looked clean enough, but there was blood on his black brogues, blood, from the knee down, on the trousers of his black suit. His white shirt and silk tie were unblemished.

Jess awoke and sat up. He shook his head so vigorously that his hair virtually obscured his face. He flinched at the sight of blood on his shirt and joined his hands together in a childish act of bemusement or contrition.

'Easter Sunday and you're praying,' Jimmy the Hat said with a lisp in his voice and a series of silent but convulsive chuckles. Jimmy the Hat was well over into his forties. Jess was a semi-professional musician. Farissey was chief pharmacist and owner of the Butetown Pharmacy. The two younger men were both thirty-eight, born on either side of the cusp between Scorpio and Sagittarius.

'Don't move off that sheet,' Jimmy the Hat whispered, wide-mouthed as if talking to deaf men. He accompanied his whisper with a series of manic hand movements. Farissey looked at the plastic sheet on which he and Jess had slept: transparent, a builder's sheet.

'JD brought us around?'

Jimmy the Hat shrugged as Farissey lit a cigarette. Jess took a dab of powder from an imitation gold case with a representation of a Bengal tiger on its face and a mirror inside: it was a prized item in Jess's extensive collection of druggie kitsch. He offered the powder around. Farissey and Jimmy the Hat silently declined.

'We could have gone back to my place. I've got all sorts of heavy-duty cleaning solvents in the pharmacy.' As Farissey spoke, a shaft of early light brightened the room. The girls on the magazine covers looked alive. He felt as though he was in an exotic aviary. His eye fell on a magazine called *Janus*. The cover showed two blonde girls in profile facing in opposite directions. The photo was cut off at the shoulders. Past and future, he wondered: desire looking both ways.

'I thought about the pharmacy,' Jimmy the Hat whispered, beating his index finger on the tip of his nose. 'But your place is too close to where it happened. Too close by half.'

'Did JD bring us here?' Jess asked, his voice metallic, nasal.

'Less you remember the better,' said Jimmy the Hat. He scurried into the front of the shop and crouched behind the till. A minute later his hand appeared over the counter like a claw. Crab-like, it scuttled around in search of the phone.

It was 7.45 when JD pulled up in the lane behind Sven Books. JAMES DWYER BUILDERS was inscribed in bold white letters on the side of his blue transit van. Jimmy the Hat opened the back door. The morning was frosty, the sun a sharp surprise in the misty sky. JD loomed silently, his bulky frame filling the door.

'You two share everything,' JD said to Farissey and Jess. His arms were folded across his powerful chest. His expression was stern, dismayed. 'Drugs, women and now someone else's blood.'

He was wearing a sheepskin jacket. His paunch looked necessary, a statement of power. He cast his eye over the room as if trying to soak up every detail. His broad face, once sharply handsome, was now distinguished with great bushy eyebrows still jet-black beneath his silver hair. Flushed with cold and melancholy exuberance, he looked like a vodka-fuelled survivor of the tundra. Big JD. At fifty-seven he was still a man to whom everyone turned in their blackest hours, even his enemies.

Jimmy the Hat carefully rolled up the plastic sheet. He and JD spread the sheet across the floor of the van; Jess and Farissey stepped into the back; slowly, mechanically. They sat mask-like, silent as mummers, as the van pulled off. Jimmy the Hat darted back into the shop, chimera-like in the harshening sun.

'I'll explain later,' JD said to Dolores at the back door of Windsor Esplanade. She wore a dressing gown whose navy blue was at odds with her Afro hairdo and light-brown skin.

'You don't need to,' Dolores said, a rasp in her waking voice. 'Some bad moons around at the moment.'

Dolores greeted Farissey with a clipped, familiar 'Jack', as mourners might do at a funeral. To Jess, she had nothing to communicate but a long, hard stare of weary outrage. She was in her early fifties, had been something of a local beauty in her youth. A part-time fortune-teller, Dolores had married JD a few years ago. It had been a second marriage for both.

She looked on with dark, amazeless eyes as the two men carefully emptied the black bags into the washing machine. Farissey and Jess walked barefoot up the stairs and took turns in a series of showers. JD washed and disinfected the plastic sheet.

By nine o'clock all four of them were taking gin and tonics as the tumble dryer rattled in the background. They'd all grown up in docks' families that survived the redevelopments in the 1960s. They agreed on a series of interlocking stories before vowing never to talk again about the events of the previous evening.

Dolores lightened the mood by telling Farissey and Jess that they were in fact both born under the thirteenth sign of the zodiac, that of Ophincus the serpent-bearer. The Ophincans are mystical, dangerous souls born in the last ten days of November. Jess listened with rapt attention: soaking it all in, memorising perhaps.

Farissey looked at Jess wearily, listened to Dolores wearily, sipped wearily on his drink. All this astrology, obeah, tarot: so many ways of mainlining spirituality. He gazed through the window on Butetown's Rat Island, an eight-street cluster of Victorian terraces which marked the area's western border with the River Taff and Grangetown. As Dolores talked of Pluto, gloomy planet of transformation, creeping over JD's moon, Farissey again wondered what this front room must mean to JD. He looked at JD's Korean War medals mounted in the glass cabinet. Then at photographs of JD's first wife and his daughter. Within these walls, JD had watched his first wife die. Within these walls, he'd mourned the death of his daughter.

'Do you know what the future means, Jack?' Dolores pushed her cheeks against their bones, to frame more certainly a gaze now direct and honest. 'It means that nothing you do will change it.'

'You could hang a thousand coats on a stand like that. You know what my future is?'

She gathered herself, drawing the energies into her field. 'It's all a jumble. Angry pools. Swirling pools. Pools where past and future get confused, everything off course; something calling to you, some test, some matter of honour. I can't see where it's coming from.'

'That's enough, love,' said JD. He bit the end from a fresh cigar.

At ten o'clock, JD enforced a two-hour drinks ban and Dolores made toast. For the remainder of the day, they would all do what they always did on a Sunday. By 12.30 Jess was on his way to do routine sound checks at the Music Factory. JD and Dolores were sitting over drinks at the Avondale. Farissey joined them some ten minutes later. He had changed into another of his black suits. Underneath, he wore a collarless beige shirt. He talked sport with JD; Dolores went to join some women friends on the other side of the bar. JD sent Dolores's drinks over to her, as was their custom. News of Christina's death was already abroad. The three expressed shock, dismay and outrage in a way that was unaffected but out of key with the excitement all around that lunchtime bar.

Everyone had something to say: a theory, a prediction, a reminiscence. It was like a carnival. Death's like that, Farissey thought. A prospect. It's festive, and no amount of hushed, respectful tones or widow's weeds, starched collars and Catholic mass cards can disguise the fact. We bid them go with poems and songs. So much more animated than the other thing: the weird isolations of birth, the retreat from the community, the singular absence of anything interesting to say about another creature grubbing its way into flesh and its time. Whereas death – well, we're all on its boat, drifting into the same port.

The story they heard that lunchtime was that two black men and a pale, dark-haired prostitute had killed Christina Villers. The men dragged the dark-haired prostitute up the stairs of the Angelina Street flat by her hair. Christina got stabbed some fifty times: her head was hanging on to her body by scrags. The white prostitute was forced to stab the dying body between its shattered ribcage. The two black men and the pale, dark-haired prostitute had formed a kind of triangle around Christina. It had to be the Baja brothers. Hadn't Christina messed them around over testifying on their behalf when they were up in court for shooting out the windows of an Indian restaurant? Also, word was around that Christina owed the Bajas a few hundred for coke. There was talk, too, of a poached deal from London.

The consensus in the bar was the Bajas would be charged but that they'd walk. When an opinion was asked of him, Farissey just said: 'They're dangerous, all right, those brothers, but I can't see them doing that.' There was a fine line between getting himself off the hook and being seen to damn the Bajas. He noted the subtle differences between the story moving around the bar and the one JD was preparing to give to DI Loudon Hargest that evening.

JD bit on the end of a cigar before lighting it. Farissey went to the bar and called the round. He added a double whisky and ginger. Back at the table, he felt an odd pain burrowing up from his shoulders on to the back of his neck. He looked around the Avondale, at the white ceiling, the fish tank. Some memory stirred in him. Here, last night, in a huge crowd, leaning against the wall, speeding, throwing down doubles and then giving over his eyes to sweat-soaked exhaustion.

Farissey finished his drinks, went back to his flat on Bute Street. His flat was above the Butetown Pharmacy: he owned the building. His living room doubled as a storeroom. Boxes of shop-front products were stacked along the walls. The front window had a stained-glass design on its upper border. It depicted some pastoral scene, perhaps Maoist. Large pictures of boxers hung on the walls. In the middle of the room there was a wooden table with gnarls and large holes. The table had belonged to Farissey's father. It had been carved by a tinker from a single piece of wood. There were no ornaments, plants or paintings. Few would suppose the flat to be inhabited by a couple, still less by two professionals.

He showered again, dressed, bandaged and disinfected his blistered fingers. He poured himself a vodka, checked his desk diary. Victoria's train from London was due into Cardiff at 7.50. That gave him time to think, time to contrive a mask. *Victoria*. Think of her so as not to think of Christina Villers. But when he tried to think of her, precisely nothing came to mind. He had no images of her, just attributes. She was his wife of four years' standing; she was a white niece to Dolores. She was a quarter black but looked more Italian than anything. Thirty-one years old, and by general consent a rare and sourceless beauty. Now a qualified lawyer, she was to begin work at Madieson and Madieson, a company which (to his consternation) were much the favoured solictors in Butetown. Victoria had vague predilections: menthol cigarettes, pasta, fish, soul music, occasional infidelities. She was pregnant, too, but had no way of telling if the child was conceived by Farissey or by Jess.

Try as he might, he could summon no image of her. All his mind was of Jess: brightly clothed, a harlequin, a trickster or tempter. Then he closed his eyes against the pounding in his head. He saw a triangle ghosting a triangle. Himself and Jess at the feet of both: Victoria and Christina Villers at the apexes.

He opened his eyes, felt oppressed by his front room, by the bars of dust motes and cigarette smoke. He felt corrosion on the air; felt the call of the estuary. He slipped a noggin of vodka into the inside pocket of his suit, and set off for the docks, hoping to walk off the strangest headache he'd ever experienced.

At seven, he came to a pause at the Queen Alexandra Dock. He leaned over the railings, lit a cigarette, tried to catch up with himself. He looked down at the water. Golden light played on its vicious, unruffled surface.

Friday night and he'd been one of four figures standing here.

Carl Baja was surveying the territory with that intelligent, remorseless gaze of his. His brother, Tony, was beside him, trying to look casual in his tacky suit, but all nervy violence inside. Carl was the king of Butetown's black underworld and had some mistaken idea that JD was his white equivalent. Carl Baja looked at JD with a mixture of threat and respect, almost as at a blanched image of the middle-aged patriarch he'd one day become. 'Where's that fucking Christina?' Baja had asked. JD looked blankly at the dock water below.

'You tell me,' JD responded. 'I leave those girls alone.'

Carl flashed a contemptuous glance at his brother. 'Me too,' Carl Baja said. He turned back to JD. 'All right. I believes you. And I also believes you'll tell me if you hear word of her.'

Farissey and JD walked on towards the town.

With every step, Farissey had felt Carl Baja's cold, weary and menacing gaze burrowing into the back of his head. Farissey felt as though that gaze was on him now as he crossed a deserted Angelina Street on his way to the central railway station.

Chapter Three

Victoria's train was running twenty minutes late. Farissey smoked a flurry of Park Drives at the platform, thinking about the early hours of that morning, of how he awoke on that plastic sheet, blood on his clothes, blood in his mind . . .

The train announcement shocked Farissey into the present. He felt dizzy as he stood at the platform, saw everything in slow motion: a hand through the window, carriage door opening, items of luggage, people unpent; all so slow that he could play over the whole pageant in reverse. People walking funereally, unspeaking, strangers all, with few to greet them.

She was among the last to get off, a taller figure in the background. He tried to see her as others might: cool, self-contained, fashionable, nameless. She was wearing an ankle-length brown coat, a black beret, an indigo scarf around which her dark hair curled. She moved gracefully, with unconscious ease. It was as though some dream or ideal drove her onwards and her body followed with the droll compliance of a lady-in-waiting.

She raised her eyes quizzically, smiled, kissed him on the cheek. He fingered her scarf. 'Looks like a sunset,' he said.

'I picked it up in Camden . . . You look terrible.'

A sly smile on her lips. She hasn't heard.

They took the quiet route, past the Glendower pub and along the line of the dried-up Glamorganshire Canal. Butetown's twilit streets felt sheltering. Under the Loudoun Square tower blocks, she told him about her fortnight in London. She complained about the endless legal dinners she had to sit through. 'It's like they let you in on condition they can confiscate your personality.' They reached the foot of Bute Street and its cluster of bars, pubs and restaurants, stopped off in Val's Bistro.

The Bistro was a narrow licensed café through which both Butetown's night and day worlds passed, as oblivious to one another as the neap and spring tides. The place was a miracle of energy, much of it coming from the lady herself, from her slender and unstinting Yemeni frame (well over into its sixties) and from eyes that burned with humanity behind sharp and angular tortoiseshell glasses. Val opened for breakfast at seven just two hours after single-handedly ushering out the last drunks, druggies and gamblers, be they eighteen-stone bruisers, impassioned Turkish guys begging for one more game of cards, a belligerent pimp and his raving girl, or the nightclub dealers arguing over the mark-up on a half-ounce of coke someone had scored up in London.

Ordinarily, he wouldn't have taken Victoria here. Whether she knew it or not, Butetown was her birthright, but not her home. It wasn't so much that something of London had left its impress on her; rather, London was always within her, waiting to find its external form. 'Beautiful, but ain't got her family's spirit,' old Butetown adjudged. One foot in two cultures, they felt. 'Be an educated type or be one of us, but don't think the two mix.' The younger women disliked her too. 'Who the fuck does she think she is, stuck-up bitch?' girls asked each other in the bars and nightclubs. They envied her those clothes twice as expensive as any worn in Butetown and two years ahead of the ever-lagging Cardiff fashions. They resented her for splitting her life between London and Cardiff as she finished her legal training. 'She'll get her comeuppance,' the girls consoled themselves. 'Good and proper.'

A waitress brought a gin and tonic for Victoria and a pint of Stella for Farissey. He drained half the glass at a single draught. 'Stayed over with JD and your Auntie Dolores last night.'

'What for?' she asked suspiciously. 'It's only five minutes away from the flat.'

Farissey fingered around his drink in search of a foreign body. 'Well, the clubs were too packed so we went back with JD to drink some whisky. Anyway, Jess has this wicked Afghani black and I just crash out on the sofa . . .'

'Jess,' she whispered. 'I thought we weren't having any more to do with him.'

'Well . . . things are so close down here.'

'I kept my half of the bargain. I told Jess I was going to make a real go of it with you and me. I only kept this triangle thing going because I thought you wanted it that way.'

'I never said I did or I didn't.'

'But that's just it,' she said, a little asperity in her voice. 'For a while, you were so distant. Whereas Jess listened to me, he cooked these elaborate meals, he spoilt me.'

And massaged you, and told you about your upcoming Saturn return, and spoke to you as though you were the queen of a thousand afternoons. I'll be everything to you, his eyes said, all sympathy and seduction. Farissey had seen him do it so many times. How could a soul put so much energy, so much of itself into these conquests, these ugly little colonisations?

'That's how Jess traps women,' he replied. 'And when they've given in, he loses interest.'

Losing interest: that had been Farissey's gambit. He could so easily have put himself between her and Jess. But he stood back, watched. Sometimes he'd wondered if something in himself longed once more to be alone with itself.

Cuckold: the two syllables once more stepped on his mind. Cuckold: the word had no resonance for him while Victoria and Jess were just having an affair of sorts. But now that she'd conceived, he felt betrayed, alone in a way that had nothing to do with solitude.

Victoria asked for a gin and tonic, made her way to the Ladies. He converted her order to a double. For himself he ordered a pint concoction of Stella, barley wine and Southern Comfort so preposterous that it took Val more time to calculate its cost than was to detain Farissey in its consumption.

As he chucked back his curious drink, the strangest feeling came over him when John Lennon's 'Jealous Guy' started up. He'd heard that song yesterday lunchtime; he and Jess drinking in here, this threatening lament curling all around their hazy talk. It chilled Farissey from the toes up rather than the neck down. He felt as though time was going into reverse and the future exploded before him as a series of so many unnecessary rehearsals.

Returning, Victoria asked why the doors had been taken off the toilet cubicles.

'Val doesn't want jumpin' jack flash in here.' Through the window, he looked up at the seagulls gathered on the rooftops, then at the queue below, waiting for fish and chips, chicken curry off the bone, burgers and kebabs.

'Terrible thing, just terrible, isn't it, Jack?' he heard Val say.

'What happened?' asked Victoria.

'You haven't heard? Young girl got stabbed to death,' Val said in those hushed and sibilant tones elderly women use when talking of the dead. 'Fifty-odd times, they say. Above the bookies on Angelina Street. She was on the game, like. But who does that sort of thing? Even animals don't. Funny thing is that I sees her getting into a taxi yesterday afternoon with a big holdall. I thinks to myself, there's a girl with trouble at her heels.'

Victoria joined the tips of her fingers beneath her chin. Her eyes followed Val as she took an order at an adjoining table.

'Did you know this prostitute, Jack?'

'Saw her around, no more. Spoke to her a few times in the North Star.'

'Why didn't you tell me?'

'I was going to, but it's just so horrible. Besides, what everyone's saying is just talk at the moment. The police haven't released any details.'

They sat in silence as debate about the murder spread from the bar area to the tables. Many of the customers seemed to accept that the Bajas were responsible if only because of their past violences. Tales of crowbarring, of blinding, of unexplained disappearances multiplied and were directly attributed to Carl and Tony Baja. Baroque hypotheses did their rounds. It was claimed that three knives were laid in triangular or even trinitarian shape about the mutilated body of the young prostitute. The numerological significance of the number three was discussed, superstition coming naturally to a community which, with its joy in human unreason, might have declared with a collective laugh: 'we would believe in God if we didn't know ourselves to be doomed from the very start.'

Talk turned to the rumour that Yardies were coming down to take over the docks. A gaunt foyboatsman attested that Christina was killed as an example to the Yardies that Butetown's Inited Idren could be trusted. 'Like they're saying: "Look, if we can kill a young girl, we can kill anyone. So you can trust us to run this patch just like you Yardies run South London." Besides, that new recruit to the Inited Idren – he's from Brixton.'

Victoria looked puzzled. 'Inited Idren? . . . That's the Rastafarian Brotherhood.'

'It was until the Bajas took over. Now it's just a front.'

'It's getting that heavy?'

'No, it isn't. That's just it.' Farissey felt like telling Val's customers this was police hysteria, that the Butetown they all shared was no more than a backwater of two-bit deals, casual intimidation, hustling and low-level protection rackets.

But he didn't speak. Instead, he followed Victoria's lead, drank up and headed for the flat, where they alternated between television and radio for more information on the murder. Christina's watch had stopped at 1.45, they heard.

'That's when her soul took flight,' said Farissey.

'That's when her body gave out,' replied Victoria, unsparingly.

She opened a box file of notes, lost interest in the news. Farissey stared into space. His limbs ached, his liver ached. He sank into agitated reverie. He thought of the sacrifice made by every prostitute. Christina gave up her body, then her blood. He emptied his mind, let it float on the silence. He needed a drink, needed the outdoors, the clean, chastening night.

He watched Victoria prepare for bed. She placed lotions on the dresser, travel money in her jacket. She cleaned her teeth with an electric brush, took a glass of grapefruit juice and soda to the bedside table.

When the bedroom light went out, he slipped downstairs, opened the door to the pharmacy. He took twenty milligrammes of valium. Back in the flat, he slugged vodka from the bottle. He debated whether to call a locum to stand in for him tomorrow morning, but knew that everything that following day should be as it usually was.

He crept into the bedroom. She was fast asleep. He sat on the side of the bed, stroked her dark hair, played patterns with it on the pillow, felt some rich sadness well up in himself. Her time in London was drawing to a close. Soon she would live in his flat, share most of his life. Yet her real being was out of his reach. He thought of his mother and father, of how two people can live entire adult lives together and yet be strangers, strangers but for the little life they'd brought into being. Victoria's words echoed in his mind: *I've got no way of telling if it's yours or Jess's.* Her guess: Jess would run a mile. His knowledge: it would be a lever for Jess; something to play with, manipulate. They determined to delay the announcement for a few months, make out she conceived a month later.

In her quiet spaces, of a child she would dream. Of that, mainly, dreamed.

The doctor's words after her abortion: *There's a chance you might not be able* . . . Wanting to be punished, she'd taken any *chance* and *might* out of it. She'd believed herself to be infertile, as had he; as, no doubt, had Jess.

He recalled when first he'd seen her. He was fifteen and helping out in his father's bar; she was a melancholy, abstracted child, sipping soft drinks silently as her mother systemically drank and drugged away the remnants of her marriage to a ship's carpenter of Norwegian ancestry. Farissey went north to study pharmacy; meantime, she was batted around between her divorcing parents and had to enlist the headmistress in her fight to stay on at school to do A-levels.

When he came back to Cardiff, she was in the midst of a breakdown, having flunked out of her law degree after a series of half-hearted yet abusive relationships. Dolores explained that the family didn't want the shame of going through the doctor. So, he gave her tricyclics but mostly he gave her time, time given on his own terms. Night by night she talked and he listened as he played out his rituals in the Butetown drink shops. Sometimes he wondered why she cleaved to him. 'You don't ask for anything from me,' she'd said. 'Someone else could be sitting beside you in a year's time and it wouldn't make a damned bit of difference.' In that ease, in that haven, they became occasional lovers, safe in different, indifferent arms.

Over the course of those soothing evenings she got better. By degrees, Farissey realised that her family's street intelligence had – in Victoria – crystallised into something more abstract, more challenging. He nurtured that uncluttered intelligence, encouraged her to complete her law degree. It was around that time they got married in a well-attended Catholic ceremony. Married, they kept each other at arm's length, never committing, never protesting. He gave over his time to the safe, undemanding solitude of bars, insomnia, night-walking. She never questioned his lifestyle; he never asked what she got up to in London.

She spent vacations in his flat, completed her degree and achieved distinctions in her postgraduate studies. Just then, though, the depression returned. Fabulous smells, she talked of, food going off, intestinal decay: something in the bedroom, the air heavy with putrefaction; something inside her rotting, sporing, tumorous, living, in motion, colonising. She'd open the windows, draw in the night air and know that the source of the smell had lodged in her nostrils: even if she found the decaying food, the bacteria remained, had bored into her, was all of her now.

One night she confessed. The bacteria was her child: child of a fellow law student in London. She'd had it aborted in London so as to avoid any fuss, any negotiation. And now, years later, she was pregnant again. About seven weeks, they estimated. But no one could be told. Not for four or five months at least: that was their secret, had to be their secret.

He closed the bedroom door silently, went back to the front room. The window beckoned, an unusual yellow glitter passing through the stained glass. Strange energies were building in him. He was restless – hours away from the tepid assuagements of valium. He gathered his keys and cigarettes, checked his crombie yet again for traces of blood. Satisfied, he made for a payphone across the street, phoned JD.

'I'm heading up to La Strella. Maybe we should have a bit of a talk?'

'Not me,' JD said. 'I'm keeping my head down until this business is straight.' Tired he sounded, stern and ashen.

'Makes sense. You pass on the story?'

'Yeah. The police bought it. Liked it, I reckon. Expect a visit.'

'Thanks, JD. Sorry for putting you in this position.'

After a long silence, JD spoke. 'I'll ask Dolores if she feels like popping up. *She wants to talk.*'

La Strella lay in a basement on Charles Street in the town centre. It was empty but for its voluptuous manageress, her bandaged legs stretched out with a tired sensuality behind the counter. The six Formica tables were laid with for-appearances'-sake cutlery in the weary and cynical game played off and on with a police as much solicitous of after-hours drink as the rest of them.

'Who's that you're with now? Related to Dolores, is she? She's beautiful.'

'I suppose she is,' Farissey replied, absently.

'I'm not being funny, Jack – don't get me wrong. But she gets to London to study and then comes back to the docks. What's all that about?'

'She wants to learn.' He flicked a lock of his dark and just greying hair from his crombie's collar as though it was a bug or flea. 'Learn what? I don't know.'

Farissey moved his glass through a circle on the counter, to mark a ritual that daily encompassed perhaps two score events like this. He didn't drink to forget nor out of exuberance. He didn't drink to escape his moods but to catch up with them. Certainly, he didn't drink to escape from himself. He drank simply to be himself, to be at home in his own body, to quell the clamour of voices in his head, to pass his days with a blank sense of self-possession. It sometimes occurred to him that he drank because his father had drunk. That his father had drunk himself into that cirrhotic hollow some quarter of a century ago was no deterrent. As many noted, there was something of the survivor in Farissey's strong, wiry frame, his tinkerish good looks.

Dolores arrived at 11.45, talked awhile to the manageress about friends dead or dying. As the club filled up, Dolores and Farissey retreated to a window table, sat before a litre of La Strella's rough wine and two gin and tonics.

'I don't want her getting mixed up in any of this. When all's said and done, she's family, and I don't want her mother hearing a whisper of this. Besides, with Victoria, you know.'

'I know,' said Farissey, dragging heavily on his Park Drive. 'She gets to hear what everyone else gets to hear.' His voice resonated heavily, even in his own head. It rose not just from a smoker's but from an addict's lungs; rose as though from some stagnant well. 'But she might well get involved anyway.'

'How?'

'Well, if the Bajas do get charged, who's going to defend them?'

Dolores removed the ice cube from her gin and tonic, sucked it. 'Madieson and Madieson – has to be,' she said defeatedly. 'No one else touches the Bajas with a bargepole . . . Why couldn't she have stuck at being a secretary or even a shopgirl?

That would have done us. All my sister and I wanted was a little good-time friend and God gives us a girl with all these high-and-mighty ideas.'

Dolores's eyes were fiery, yet drained, as though they had looked too deep and too long at something cankerous, hidden and subterranean. Farissey prospected that beautifully weary and wise face, noble where most it was vulnerable, and thought how little he knew the soul under its animations. He wondered was it this image he loved beneath its niece's dauntless and avid evasions.

Farissey walked Dolores home, walked home himself, repudiated the idea of home. He looked at the low sky as at a cope, a screen, a blankness on which his memory might weave its secret patterns.

The night held no terrors for him; never had. He stepped on to Bute Street, felt that incomparable silence of a deserted main drag. As he turned into Angelina Street, he was eyed suspiciously by two policemen in a stationary car. He was no longer a pharmacist, a citizen, but a solitary male in the watchful night. His memory now had craters. His soul had craters.

He passed on towards the traffic lights. Police signs and blinding lights in the flat above the bookmakers. Forensics, he supposed. The room held secrets, mysteries, invisible traces like those carved on Christina's retina, carved on her pulse. 1.45: the time her watch would always tell. Was it the shock to her body or the flight of her soul that stilled those hands? What hand turned the time, moved around the dream?

The police car flashed its lights at him. He turned back into Bute Street, walked the ways of his childhood. He wanted the voice to fill him, the voice he mistook for prayer or grace. He was overcome by forces that were neither light nor dark. He thought with the imagined voice of the city, of its good, its just, its ancestral desire.

Say it and say it now, the city said. Say it and wander miles and miles of fetid and sullen dockyard lanes, thread your memory like a silver trail through that strange and most recent of nights. Say the name now, like your mother might have, with her gravelling and graveyard timbre. Say it like you should have when hostage to banister and rope with cigarettes fireflied into your childish skin. Say it, black gangster, urban ghost, white stalker, pants-creaming halfwit. Say it yourself, myself, whoever you are.

Say it and say it now.

A city calls to your name.

Chapter Four

Careful not to disturb Victoria, Farissey awoke at 7.45 a.m. It was three days after the murder. He lit a Park Drive, measured out a double vodka, drank it while he bathed. He showered, shaved, measured another double, mixed it with tonic for rapid absorption. He drank the second double as he dressed. He corrected shaving irregularities, brushed down his black suit and tied a Windsor knot into his tie. He applied two types of mouthspray and took twenty milligrammes of ephedrine to counteract any drowsiness from the twenty milligrammes of valium he had taken last thing at night. He then prepared a quadruple vodka and tonic in a plastic bottle and secreted it behind the cistern of the upstairs lavatory.

He walked down the narrow staircase and opened his pharmacy. He placed one bottle of mouthspray in a drawer, made two cups of coffee and awaited the arrival of his assistant. He'd followed these steps for more than ten years as owner and chief pharmacist of the Butetown Pharmacy. No one had ever seen him the worse for wear. They wouldn't. He knew his body would give out long before his mind.

He set himself to book-keeping and answered the odd query

about whether certain medicines were compatible. He came to the front of the shop to inspect mild wounds, rashes caused by reactions to medicines or lotions. A woman came in with conjunctivitis; an adolescent with candida crumbling away his fingernails.

The pharmacy was busy that morning, mainly with customers buying over-the-counter products. Old men and women in vulturine coats talked of the murder. No matter what kind of a life she'd lived, she was a young girl, no more than that, and – who knows? – with the right parents or the right whatever, well, she could be a new mother now, but what sort of a man could do such a thing? Well, no man neither; even wolves don't do that to their own. On and on they talked, strident and raucous like jackdaws.

Farissey was on the verge of telling them to do their talking somewhere else when a fat, bearded Valleysman came into the shop in a state of severe anxiety. Farissey took his pulse and blood pressure. Beads of sweat fell from the man's face onto Farissey's hands. He administered fifteen milligrammes of intravenous diazepam and called a locum. The valium only tempered the anxiety. The locum arranged for the Valleysman to be admitted to a psychiatric ward. Farissey observed the process with frustration. He suggested to the locum that the anxiety might derive from coronary dysfunction.

At eleven, he felt his concentration flagging. He swept upstairs and drank off the vodka preparation in the lavatory of his flat. He applied more mouthspray and some deodorant. The whole process took less than three minutes.

During the afternoon, his assistant passed through a prescription for lorazepam. Lorezepam-Ativan was an alien invasion, he explained to his assistant. There was no withdrawal like it. The body had a genetic memory of heroin and alcohol, based as they were on the poppy, the grain or grape. That memory made withdrawal feverish but familiar, less intense and in step with the rhythms of nature. He made up the prescription none the less, told the customer to ask her GP about possible alternatives.

Late in the afternoon, he felt his mood plummet. The greying of the day got mixed in with his mood. He set himself to mechanical stocktaking. With the close of business, he felt both tremulous and relieved.

He stood at the window of his flat. The shakes were imminent, frosty fingers crawling around his brain and neck and arms. He was out of tonic water, needed the bubbles to get the drink the quicker into his head. He washed down three fingers of vodka with a bottle of Pils. He went to the kitchen window, waited for his being to steady itself out. As he looked, some memory of blood and chaos and shouting was trying to rise in him. He went into the front room, lit a cigarette at the window. A police car pulled up outside the entrance to the pharmacy. Farissey was already downstairs when the three heavy knocks sounded on the door.

He opened the door to two plain-clothes policemen. One he recognised as DI Loudon Hargest, a giant of a man in his mid-fifties who always seemed to be holding some fury in precipitous check. He had a huge pockmarked face and small, bright, intuitive eyes. Hargest had been on a crusade against Carl Baja for more than a decade, thought himself a rationalist to whom nothing was personal. But Butetown knew that Hargest personalised everything. Like a cuttlefish, he gave out emotional signals by changes in colour.

Hargest wanted information about clients at the pharmacy: paranoid types, schizophrenics. As Farissey invoked confidentiality, the red of Hargest's face turned to puce, the light blue of his shirt collar turned royal with sweat. The detective stayed silent awhile, grinding away at his teeth.

Hargest asked if he might look around in Farissey's flat. He went to the living-room window, which looked on to the east side of Bute Street. He poked around in the boxes of shop-front products. Hargest remarked on the wooden table.

'Not very practical, is it?' Hargest put a finger in one of its many holes.

'My father's table.'

Hargest wanted to look around the kitchen. The other policeman wandered into the main bedroom, opened drawers, clattered coat-hangers along their rails. Hargest inspected the black cooking range and opened the door of the empty washing machine. Through the kitchen window, they prospected the murder flat on Angelina Street. The bookies below had closed until police inspections and forensics were complete.

Farissey looked at the door of the flat, tried to see what the schoolgirl had seen. A report on the radio at lunchtime said that she'd woken up with a bad stomach and saw a man in his thirties crouched in the lane behind the bookies. He had, she said, lank hair, and was wrapped in a black duffel coat. Farissey saw this wreck of a man, folded into himself, wringing blood from his hands. Could Farissey himself have seen it in reality? This spent, shocked and huddled figure? Or was it just wishful thinking – a redeeming, penitent image?

'Did you see anything last Saturday?' Hargest asked. His voice was sonorous, heavy.

'I wasn't here. I stayed over with some friends.'

'Ah, now, isn't that a pity? With a view like this, well, you could have seen everything. Here in the dark, a drink in your hand, just watching, soaking it all up.'

Hargest took a note of names and addresses.

'You know JD anyway,' Farissey protested.

'Do I know anyone? Really? Do you? Sometimes on this fucking job, I don't think anybody even knows themselves.'

Farissey smelled rich, sticky sweat on the air. Hargest would have smelled something different. Digested muscle tissue gave to Farissey's breath a pear-like bouquet, exhaled now in a flood of smoke.

'How about Jess Simmonds? Does he bring prescriptions in here?'

'I don't believe he's seen a doctor in his life,' Farissey replied. He looked at Hargest in all his eighteen stones, at the huge neck, the barrel chest. He saw him as some dull, tense, jeopardised beast; meaning things all the time, mutely, primitively meaning. Always a shock to see a big man racked with nerves, poignant almost.

'Did you see our darker brethren in the Avondale?' Hargest

came closer, loomed over him. Farissey wasn't used to being dwarfed, but Hargest was all of six foot four inches and eighteen stones of muscle; his Adam's apple like a ball-bearing and a neck you'd scarcely get your hands around.

'The Baja brothers?' Hargest insisted when Farissey affected incomprehension.

'No,' Farissey said. 'Someone said Carl was working the door at the Casablanca.'

'What do you think of Carl Baja?'

Farissey paused, lit another Park Drive from his Zippo lighter. 'Sure I was frightened of him at school. We all were. Even at fourteen he was over six foot and built like a heavy-weight. He looked more deadly than Sonny Liston did in his heyday; too big and ponderous to be Tyson. That kind of weary, awesome look Liston had. But for all that, Carl had a sensitivity, a sort of compassion.'

'Compassion?'

'Yeah, just that.' When both were teenagers, Farissey had seen Carl Baja in St Cuthbert's Church. Baja was kneeling in the otherwise empty church like a stilled beast, his hands clasped in seemingly rapt prayer.

'Do you think he could have killed this prostitute?'

'If it was a dealer or club owner or something, then I'd say "maybe". But I can't see him killing a woman.'

'One day, perhaps you will,' Hargest said, a softness creeping into his voice. 'We'll need to interview you formally in the week. Use that memory of yours. People say you remember everything. Clever soaks often do.'

On the way out, Hargest looked at the looming photographs of boxers: Tommy Farr, Jack Dempsey, Jimmy Driscoll.

'My father's pictures.'

'All bones now, but what stories those pictures could tell, h'm? Bravery, fear, cowardice, thrown fights, who knows? I remember them from the House of Blazes. We drank there in the 1950s, when me and JD were back from Korea. You'd have been a baby. He kept a good bar, your old man. Pity he didn't keep himself better.' Hargest cast him a look that Farissey couldn't figure –

something between concern and menace and somehow more than either.

'Oh, by the way,' he continued, 'we're going to put the prostitute that found the body under hypnosis. You know her – Lida Varaillon. She's entitled to a witness. You're the only professional she knows. I don't suppose you'll refuse.'

'I don't suppose I will.'

'And I doubt you'd object to hypnotherapy yourself.'

'I doubt I would.'

Farissey stood at the top of the staircase as the officers left. On the way out, Hargest asked if he wanted a witness. Farissey shrugged, shook his head, smiled. He went into the kitchen, poured a vodka and opened a bottle of lager.

Through the kitchen window he saw Jess Simmonds draped along the fire exit. Jess was wearing a floral shirt and biker's jacket. His long blond hair fell sleekly on to his shoulders. There was some gloating laughter in his eyes. Farissey thought of that Rossetti painting: lovers at the bridge meeting their doubles, their shadow selves.

'Well?' Jess asked as Farissey stepped out on to the fire exit.

'He'll be coming to see you. Informal at first. Then he'll drag us in for formal interviews. He's going to put me under hypnosis. I trotted out the story. A few drinks, no drugs, everyone feeling good but not drunk. You'd better clean up your flat. But leave some draw and a few dabs around or he'll think you're taking the piss.'

'It's easy enough for you, Jack.'

'That's because I'm legitimate and you're illegitimate. We all make choices, Jess.'

'Come on, Jack, play the white man. You know I didn't have much of a choice in school.'

Jess reached into the inside pocket of his leather jacket. He packed a purple and white hash pipe, one of the twenty or so he'd gathered on his travels. He lit it leeringly, offered Farissey a hit. Farissey looked back at him with leaden impatience.

'Well, we're bonded again, Jack. You and me – just like the old days.'

'You'd better get along. The less we're seen around each other, the better,' Farissey said, leaning out of the window. He held his vodka tumbler in his hand like a weapon. Some perverse wish came upon him to squeeze his hand into the glass, show Jess some image of mutilation, a bloodied talon.

'Sure, Jack, but consider this. Who remembers more about Easter Saturday?'

Jess swaggered down the dull prospect of the fire exit. Something feline in his step, as though the eyes of all the world were on his every move. He was bluffing, Farissey knew. But he knew also that Jess's intent was darker, deeper, more unfathomable than anything to do with the law or ordinary retributions.

Farissey continued looking out over the fire exit long after Jess had departed. A lost mood stole over him, something like that springtime dusk over the canal when he and Jess had pierced one another's ears with a needle, dabbed the wounds with meths. They'd have been fifteen at most. It wasn't that long after Jess started collecting and washing glasses at the House of Blazes. Jess was doing a flurry of other jobs, too. He was helping his mother manage the Butetown Aquarium, doing paper rounds, odd jobs for builders and decorators, running for bookies. He was mitching off school to help on a tugboat three days a week. His sister was helping out the mother, doing piece-work when she could. Brother and sister spent the odd evening distributing pools coupons.

Butetown figured that Jess's father wasn't providing, felt vindicated when Jess's father left his family a few months later. No one remarked on how odd it was, then, that Jess went back to school at precisely that time. His sister stopped doing piece-work, Jess gave up all his odd jobs, his work on the tugboat.

Loss would unite the two boys when Farissey's father died of cirrhosis shortly afterwards. They lived with forgetful intensity, lived in a contumacious and unspoken adolescent contract. Hour upon hour, they played pinball in darkened afternoon cafés like ghosts in arm. They whiled away sunsets on the banks of the Glamorganshire Canal, drank flagons of Brains Dark in the half-lights of the aquarium. They communicated with such rare intensity that conversation became sparse between them. They seemed to meld into a single being. Farissey heard Jess's voice with that embarrassed recognition he felt hearing his own on a tape recording. On occasion, he tried to escape Jess's influence, but he was drawn back. He knew they were banded beyond good and evil, beyond convenience or desire. Even in hatred, they were brothers.

Hatred had united them in the form of the gangs that grew up in the 1960s when the town planners cleared the docklands. Out of eyes that had never seen beyond books, suburbs, maps, ministerial briefings and theses on planned societies, the far-flung estates emerged like fabulous and grotesque birds taking wing from the encyclopaedia. Each spawned its own army of disconsolates who'd make night pilgrimages to set fire to shops and smash windows when their petty arsenals of flick knives, low-grade incendiary devices and glass-beaded knuckle-dusters couldn't be deployed against the other gangs. But the docks' gang reigned supreme and, their families having survived demolitions and rehousing, Farissey and Jess were drawn into the gang by the promise of drugs and springtime girls only to find themselves unable to leave when it all turned to tedium and a daily round of grinding fear.

'Once you're in with us there's no out,' Carl Baja had told them, and Farissey and Jess lived the terror of inside and outside until three deaths one summer spelled the temporary dis-banding of the 110-strong Butetown army. The two friends slipped out of a world which would have seen them kicked to pieces, expelled from their schools and dragooned to the crim's apprenticeship of borstals and joblessness.

As adults, they'd play over the violences with a grim nostalgia: a greaser's head smashed forty times into the concrete of a park's play area before the Roath boys took him into an alley and kicked him half to death; Carl Baja twisting that skinhead's eye clean out of its socket with a broken milk-bottle. In another mood, they'd relive the desperate and threatened early loves they'd found on those derelict evenings. Too many shots in common, too many tatty postcards of times past, too many shared faces forgotten by day but stringed like marionettes through dreams and psychedelic reverie to leave their souls unbonded.

Farissey's mind returned to the unreality of the present. He pulled on his black crombie, checked the collar yet again for any staining. He went down to the pharmacy, cleared outstanding business on his desk. As he walked up Bute Street towards the town bars, a pile of newspapers under his arm, he wondered if this rivalrous bond was all that either of them owned.

Chapter Five

With her dark-brown hair in a ponytail, and hands folded demurely in her lap, Lida Varaillon looked more like a pretty, troubled child than a drug-addicted hustler or the 'pale, dark-haired prostitute' of media reports. Under interview, she would tilt her head slightly to the left when giving a question serious consideration and look up and around the room when bored. She also had a disconcerting habit of resting her head on her left shoulder almost as though she were asleep. She avoided eye contact for the most part, but when returning a gaze Lida did it intently with oceanic, hazel-brown eyes. A lover's look almost, one which challenged you to prove that you were not within her, in some watery home or grave she'd made for you.

Farissey sat now in a luminous room high in the Central Police Station. It lay in Cathays Park, a civic space of creamy-white buildings, parkland and broad vermilion avenues. Some ten officers were assembled. Lida sat at a long table placed in front of the window. Three hours ago, her hypnosis session had drawn a complete blank on the circumstances of Christina's murder. Farissey's hypnotherapy had taken place the previous evening: at his own request, it went by without independent witness.

Mellow spring light flooded the room as Hargest arranged his notes. He craned forward from his chair, asked Lida to clarify her relationship with the murdered prostitute.

Christina was Lida's best friend. She was twenty, a year older than Lida and more experienced. She'd introduced Lida to the Butetown scene, eased her into the streetwalking life. Lida rented the barren Angelina Street flat for the occasional punter who wanted a bed. Things had started to go wrong in Christina's relationships. Also, she was getting too pally with the coppers. She was playing two sides off against each other, and Lida sensed that trouble was around the corner. So, when Christina had said she needed a hideaway, Lida didn't ask her who or what she was fleeing. She simply gave the spare keys to her friend and promised to pop in every other day. The flat was only a stone's throw from Lida's council house in Sanqhar Court. They had a code. If the curtains were open, Lida knew the flat was empty. When closed, it meant that Christina was either sleeping or entertaining a punter.

At 1.45 that morning, Lida was doing another line of speed in her house in Sanqhar Court. The window was open. She heard screams travelling the seventy yards from the open window of the Angelina Street flat. When she got into the room, Christina was covered in blood and pawing at the window. Both brothers had bloody knives in their hands. They were arguing. 'If you don't know how to treat a fucking woman, I'll show you,' Carl shouted at his younger brother. Everything seemed to go into slow motion then. Christina's hands slid from the window, her body slid to the floor. She was beyond screaming, but still Carl Baja went back at her with the knife. He then turned on Lida herself, smeared Christina's blood on to her blouse. Baja then gave Lida the knife and forced her to stab Christina.

'Carl Baja in control of it all,' Loudon Hargest said. 'And where exactly did he make you stab her?'

'Under her ribs at first.'

'Was her ribcage exposed?'

'There was two T-shirts she had on, still on her, but they was covered with blood and shredded sort of like lace. A wad of fat was sticking out. Tina's eyes – they went out some time around then. Maybe she moaned a little longer, but it wasn't Tina any more. It wasn't my friend; she was gone.'

A tremor came into Lida's voice, a shadow into her look. Whether it was the truth or not, there could be little doubt that the image was now in front of her eyes, experienced as reality.

'No one could have led her on that, could they?' Hargest whispered to a nearby woman officer. 'That's all forensics.'

Lida said nothing, kept her eyes fixed in front of her. She tilted back in her chair, shivered a little in her white T-shirt and blue jeans.

'It's so unlucky, Lida, love,' Hargest continued. 'So unlucky and so bad for a young girl like you to be caught up in a mess like this. See, how are the Bajas going to trust you not to witness against them? That's why Carl puts a knife into your hand – the knife he'd used on her – and they both force you to cut her wrists and prod around under her ribcage and then they force you to poke around in her neck – and there wasn't any of it left, was there? Just a few fibres holding it to her shoulders. But she wasn't even quite dead then. There was some last gasp, and that made you feel like you'd done it, you'd given her the killing touch. But you shouldn't feel guilty, we know that, because *the Bajas made you complicit* – isn't that right? – by making you put a knife in your friend's wounds.'

Made you complicit, Farissey thought. The implication was tripping on Hargest's tongue. *Just like we can* . . .

Lida shrugged, lit a cigarette, swung her leg over the side of her chair. 'Can I go home to my baby soon?'

'In about three hours,' Hargest replied. 'A WPC will take you for lunch in the canteen. Then you can rest for an hour before you make your formal statement.'

Lida began shaking in a series of stifled sobs. Unbidden, she spoke. 'That's all Tina cared about. She was jealous 'cause I've got this new baby. She has this thing, too, about her mother fucking off when she was little. She used to get all upset and say

"No one will ever love me – even my mother fucked off" and I'd say "Everyone fucks off, Tina, sweetheart, even kids will in the end".'

By 1.30, the room had cleared but for Farissey and Hargest. The latter was motionless but for crunching his mandibles. Immense tiredness was in the detective's eyes. He invited Farissey to the table, opened a large box file, spread its contents.

'Why's Lida saying all this?' asked Farissey. 'Her hypnosis didn't reveal a thing. When she got to the night of the murder, she saw nothing.'

'I'll give you two avenues of interpretation, Jack,' Hargest said, evidently pleased with his phrase. 'First: hypnotherapy is bollocks. Second: hypnotherapy is not bollocks. We've done two interviews with Jess Simmonds. If I add them to what we dredged up under hypnosis you'll understand the sort of case we can build against you.'

Farissey fell silent. He looked at Hargest, at a face never young, a face still pockmarked and acne-scarred. His mind went back twenty or more years to the gangdays, days when Hargest was the only copper the docks' boys feared. Even in those lost gangdays, Hargest was a man so exactly himself that time could do no more than accrete around him as if around an iron stake.

Farissey broke the silence. 'What did I say under hypnosis?'

'Who's interviewing who here? I wouldn't rush the issue, if I were you. The transcript doesn't make pretty reading.'

Hargest paused, suppressed a belch. He drew attention to a note at the top of the box file: 'Christina Villers, 20 years, 5′ 3″, no distinguishing marks, a small foetus in her womb, carrying aspermic semen probably deposited three hours before her death, blood type ABO.'

'Aspermic,' Hargest said. 'I suppose you know what that means.'

'Something like non–alcoholic beer?'

'Just so, Jack. Just so.'

*

Over the course of the next thirty minutes, Farissey pondered the circumstances surrounding the murder of Christina Villers. Expected to testify in a court case on the Bajas' behalf, she failed to present herself. Word was also out that she was a police informer. She owed the Bajas a few hundred for cocaine. Needing her alive to testify at the retrial, and alive and earning to repay the coke debt, the Bajas supposedly decided to make a point to the hustlers and the pimps and the dealers by killing her in a frenzied attack which ran entirely counter to the ethos of an exemplary gangland slaying.

Still, Farissey thought, anyone can do anything on enough drugs whether they think of themselves as sophisticated gangsters or not. The brothers are bad and this concern with the 'real' killer walking the streets didn't make sense, for where's the sense in having everyone out on the streets, this lunatic, this 'Mr X' *and* the Bajas, and if that was justice, well, wouldn't we all be better off without it?

He wondered awhile but another mood was taking him over as he read that Christina dreamed only of having a baby. For all the chaos, the hustling and the drugs, she'd always been organised about condoms and contraception. She wanted to do this properly. Find herself a proper boyfriend, make enough money to get off the streets, out of the docks, into a house that she and some trustworthy bloke might own. Straighten out, the pair of them. Make him a proud father.

There were two prospectus-sized white envelopes amid the documentation marked PHOTOGRAPHS and POLAROIDS. Farissey leafed through the photographs, looking for changes, degeneration: a hardening around the lips, a blankness in her eyes. But there was no essential change. What was more, in each and every picture, this surprisingly innocent face – mopped a little clownishly in strawberry-blonde frizzes – had taken on a peculiarly imploring quality, as though the young prostitute's eyes were beseeching him, Jack Farissey, to listen for the truth of those few hours between Christina getting into a taxi near Argyll Square and the last cries of Lida Varaillon's recent testimony.

He opened the envelope marked POLAROIDS. He saw the

plastic earrings, patent slip-ons, blue jeans and black leather jacket of the vulnerable little toughie, two shredded and blood-rimed T-shirts, three condoms sentinelled at the head of the mattress, half-smoked butts and a roach bent into the ashtray, a speed-traced make-up mirror, black eyelining brushes, two phone cards, walls splattered with blackening scarlet, once blood.

He studied the shots again, trying to see with another eye. He wanted to cross the line that separates the detective from his quarry. He wanted to see as a killer sees.

Doers rarely see the full range of the deed and its outcomes. Rarely are they arrested by the primal intricacies of neckbones, the sight of how flesh falls and sunders and sags, loosehangs and flaps or flitters, like scythed wallpaper. Rarely do they taste deep in the gut the sheer stench that grows from it many hours after the bowels have blown and the whole scene has been composed, serene and implacable like a still of destiny, never again to be shifted in the tiniest detail, like a painting made not by human hand but the mind itself, the groundkeeper's football stadium at midnight, a camera still running after the riot, the absconded God oblivious to its world and wake.

Hence the desperate contracts of hunter and quarry, detective and murderer: a brutalised body unites as it divides them. One knows a before, the other an after. The murderer is on the side of life, the detective with death. One lives among fear, animation, frenzy and the blood singing. The other is swamped in stagnancies, charnel, silence, a stillness that must be charmed back into life, into death-dealing life. Few are the killers who dwell among their dead: Nielsen an exception here and hence his lament that what outraged was not so much his slaughter of the young, the hapless and the dispossessed, but – like that novelist given to dining with the characters of his creation – his watching of television, his drinking of tea amid their remains.

What mind recalled that look in her eyes, what face found itself returned in that look, framed and lost by her eyes as the skewered body relinquished vision? What undreamed-of alchemies might restore the image of the killer like those grainy bars of a prison cell restored from the cornea of that hanged man who bequeathed to the world its primordial photograph? What mind recalled, what mind wondered?

He felt it there and then. This was the work of one mind, not of two or more. The police were right. The Bajas were killers, that he knew. But not *her* killer.

He said as much to the returning Hargest. The latter dismissed the idea with a wave of his hand. 'Maybe you did stumble across something that night. But that doesn't mean you did anything, does it?'

Farissey looked over transcripts of the interviews with Jess. They were conducted according to a strategy that was simple but deadly in its results. Jess thought he was being guided to incriminate Farissey along a you-or-him line, while all the time the police were leading him away from the idea of Mr X, the solitary psychopath. Jess claimed that – around 1.30 – he'd been separated from Farissey, who had said: 'I'm going to sort out that fucking prostitute.'

In his second interview, Jess maintained that Farissey was 'off his head' but now had him saying '*they're* going to sort out that fucking prostitute'. It was likely, Jess said, that Farissey had slipped off to urinate when the Bajas left the murder flat. Carl Baja was shouting: 'We've taught that piece of fuckmeat a lesson – real good this time.'

Hargest folded his hands together. 'You see, Jack, my feeling is this. You were in that room. But you were too far out of your head to have done a thing.'

'Truth is, I can't remember a thing after about one in the morning.'

Hargest then turned to activities on Angelina Street on the morning of Christina's murder. He centred his questions on the possibility of confused recall. Farissey said that he'd seen the Bajas on Angelina Street in the middle of a skirmish.

'It was chaos: twenty-odd people near the flat, people sitting on cars, people shouting. Most were black, or blackish, but not all. A fight broke out between two prostitutes. I haven't got names for them. One of them was screaming: "He's my pimp, he's not your fucking pimp. I'll tear your fucking clitoris out, darling." Anyway, I feel so bad at this point, I just sit down in a shop doorway. I look up and the fight's still going on, but the Bajas aren't there any more.'

'What was Carl Baja's point of departure on Angelina Street?'

'I don't know where he went.'

'So it's possible that he went into 21 Angelina Street?'

'Yes.' Farissey conceded the logical point. 'But only to the extent that I can't say it's impossible.'

'Good.' Hargest jotted down a few notes. 'What do you know of the Yardie infiltration of Butetown?'

'I wasn't aware there had been one.'

'One member of Inited Idren is from Brixton.'

'Primo, right? But he's got cousins here. He's been visiting since he was a kid.'

'Is Carl Baja associated with Yardies in London or Birmingham?'

'I wouldn't know. But I doubt it very much. As far as I understand it, the Yardies cleaned up in South London because they shot first and asked questions later. They pre-empted everything. Carl isn't like that. He can be terrifying, but he has to have some sort of grievance.'

'How about Tony Baja?'

'I doubt he'd be stupid enough to make connections behind Carl's back.' Hargest sat up, drummed his fingers on the table as if rhythmically calling his speech to mind. 'You understand my concerns. Butetown is going to be one of Europe's major sites of redevelopment. This area can't look anything but spick and span if the hard cash is going to come in. Now me, I don't give a fucking monkey's whether they make it the Venice of the North or not. But this area is overdue for another clean-up. The rule of law and order will be seen to apply.'

Hargest closed the interview a few minutes later. He shook Farissey's hand, held it just that bit longer than was required.

*

Hargest was striking a deal, so much Farissey knew as he walked through the town centre. The detective was under pressure for a swift conviction. Usually, only a *series* of prostitute killings would warrant such intense investigation. Farissey thought of the DRC, the Docklands Regeneration Corporation. Clearly, it wielded more power than he had supposed.

Butetowners had reacted with scepticism when, two years ago, the DRC began promoting 'Cardiff Bay' as a northern Venice or European Seattle, promising that it would be 'Europe's most exciting waterfront'. Quiet assurances had been made that the redevelopments would provide employment for the local people. With the murder of Christina Villers, however, the DRC was confronting an area which it presumed was not only hellbent on its own destruction but that of a corporate city already coming to think of itself as 'the world's youngest capital'. After all, Christina not only lived in Butetown but was killed there and by its own black gangsters. Farissey recalled how – last summer – the DRC began to talk up the proposed bypass as providing 'unmediated access to the waterfront' which most took to mean that the mythical tourists would escape the threatening length of Bute Street, the oppressions of the Loudoun Square tower block, the maze of little council houses or the raw and loud street life where Bute Street splintered into Angelina Street and Mount Stuart Square.

Farissey recalled the promotional photography for 'Cardiff Bay': all sparkling white youth, smiling anaemic businessmen, sprightly, white old age. The promise of redevelopment seemed less an attempt to rejuvenate than to raze a community with its own, self-regulating and irregular forms of justice and peacekeeping. With the murder of Christina Villers, the authorities were now ready to go into open war with the creole life of Butetown.

Of course, it had always been that way. Even as the longromanced Tiger Bay, the area had sat at the southernmost point of the city like a restless and imponderable secret, a primal source of land or fortune whose existence must ever be disowned like a distant forebear who sweated, soiled, risked his life –

murdered even – so that successive generations might prosper. Those generations soon fled the living ground of their prosperity and, with the arrival of West Indian and African immigrants after the First World War, the isthmus was not only regarded as a slum but also a warren of evil byways, of sordid sexual encounters, open drug-taking, poisonous ethnic cuisine and darktown atrocity. Inhabitants were shamed into accepting that they lived 'below the bridge', almost as if below a species line.

The Cardiff respectable took no account that they lived 'above': they simply did not think of Butetown, still less pass over into a place where they were assured that knives were freely wielded and black men crouched in alleys or cul-de-sacs ready to pounce for money or worse. By the 1970s, and with the terminal decline of the docks, the descendants of these great migrations and miscegenations found themselves as used up as the abandoned canals and wharfs, the rusting foundries and downscaling steelworks. Redundant as well as disreputable in the post-industrial age, they simply lived on: the spent residue of a dream dreamed by someone else.

The law of the land ends here, Farissey thought as he passed under the heaviness of the Bute Street Bridge which separated Butetown from the city proper. Long ago, those words were on his father's tongue whenever they returned from some shopping expedition in the city centre.

Farissey was just about old enough to remember those days before the Tiger departed its Bay. He was eleven or twelve when the redevelopments began in 1963, remembered keenly those sheltering streets in the late '50s. He was, then, seven and eight years old and the king of his days. He knew his memory played him false, that the time was glorified by a child's recall of a few scenes, a black man mechanically strumming a guitar, an aura of urban magic.

He remembered how you could see, of a sundown, the Irish warming to their drinking and their cards' 45s in his father's bar; the Chinese outback of their laundries and lost at the end of opium pipes or dicing or marvelling at the fire of numbers in the lottery of paku pu or the ornate and shell-based mysticism of fan-tan. How the Italian women would hang out of windows shouting incomprehensible angers at one another from above ice-cream shops and cafés, just a block away from Somalis slaughtering goats on a street corner. He remembered, too, his father telling him of the fifty or so brothels the police passed by with no more than a discreet sideways glance into those dank and gloomy caverns with their own seas and treacheries for the paid-off seamen who might awake from week-long drunks to be crimped or shanghaied, perhaps in the early scalds of gonorrhoea, and aboard a vessel bound, like as not, for northern Spain or the Ivory Coast.

Farissey was old enough to still have in his ears the spectacular noise, of cockatoos, penny-slot pianos, of hurdy-gurdies, irrepressible Breton onion sellers, West Indian newspaper touts and stentorian fish hawkers. Old enough to have the taste in his nostrils of what he thought was 'tarmac' until he was old enough to say 'tarpaulin' and know that it came from shipping chandlers in a bay and a dock where the flags of a dozen or more nations fluttered with a thousand coastal birds and cooking smells in the sea breezes.

He remembered those severe winter mornings when his father took him to see the leviathan-like ships coming in from the world over to a West Dock often so congested that a trained monkey might cross from one side to the other by swinging on the masts of ships. He'd learned the places of the world from vessels and cargoes, and the world's religions from the Greek Orthodox Church, the mosques of Maria Street and Peel Street, the Norwegian Church with a dome like a witch's hat and the abiding and gruesomely iconic cross of St Mary's Church, where the women who looked like they were in fancy dress would gather with mischief, easy sacrileges and good business sense at eight o'clock of an evening.

A place withal where he'd never been but still a vast circus on this small ghetto whose ghosts still danced and cried and laughed and cried in Farissey's reveries as he now walked past the stone seasons of Loudoun Square and alongside the twelve-foot wall (so grim as to seem penal) that separated the local railway line from the east side of Bute Street.

It all changed in the early 1960s. The town planners determined to clear the slums in a dream of enforced integration. They relocated the ethnic groups on some such principle that sharing a corridor, a landing, a defective lift, an estate park and dismal, steel-shuttered shopping centre was altogether more propitious than melding on an exuberant, rank and impossibly variegated main drag. It was carnival that frightened them, Farissey knew: the sight of a creole community evolving its own way of being, its own ethics of spontaneity, respect and cheerfulness – without need of statute, politician or book – like a city shrived of politics or dignitary and mirthed into its own order by jokers, acrobats and fakirs.

The dead hand got working a quarter of a century ago when the sheltering alleyways of his youth were replaced by tower block and cul-de-sac. Why should anyone care if it looked like some maritime Disneyland in ten years' time, a cultural museum, as without people as walls, its clocks and traffic lights turning the time?

Chapter Six

The following weeks passed slowly as the arrest of the Baja brothers hung over Butetown. Days of brightness alternated with unbroken cloud. Strong sunshine gave Butetown the depthless and disappointed luminosity of white gravel; grey days simply played strophe to the antistrophe of paving and brick, tower block and courtyard. The only constant was a breeze low or dropped altogether so that it seemed that either the seagulls had fled from the close horizons or that the elements held the steady soundtrack of their cawing in some channel of air just beyond the shoreline. The natural silence served to remind the eye of the hard, grassless, concreted, white expanse of Butetown. A few seemingly sapless trees grew from the pavements in small rectangles of pebbled mud. Appearing at regular intervals alongside the tower blocks and council houses, the trees added to the bleak, unlandscaped monotony, answerless, as they were, to rain, breeze, flowering or season.

On the first Saturday of May, Butetown achieved some amnesty with the city proper as an iconoclastic cover-band called the Racketeers lit up the Big Windsor with twisted versions of old classics like 'Mystery Train' and 'Baby, Please Don't Go'. Dolores and JD jived a few numbers amid neo-hippie students. Dealers patrolled the corridors, peaceably in search of trade. Docks' boys gathered in smoke-sanctified mystery around the balconies.

A few hustlers stationed themselves in the corridors like so many zombified and draped pretties. A woman of about twenty-five paraded through the main bar in a floor-length split black leather coat that opened on to soft black stockings, black ankle bands and stilettos. She entered as if bringing the night air with her. A precise face was curled and framed by a black bob, eyes promising sex and more than sex. Looking but not looking: a studied and impenetrable art.

Farissey stood on a balcony among hard white guys with tattoos, solemn Rastas and crop-headed bad boys. He was wearing a dark-blue suit, a white shirt and silk tie patterned in black and red. He had a pint in one hand, a chaser in the other; a cigarette in his mouth which he was not so much smoking as wearing down. He had a strange quality of being absolutely at home and impassively remote in that gathering. But for his ever-watchful eyes, he had that dreamy, immovable quality of a statue amid pageants and sightseers.

The talk around him was of the arrests. Tony Baja had been apprehended in Acram's pool hall. The police allowed him to finish his game. He'd come out joking with them; told his mates to expect him back in a couple of hours. Carl Baja had been another matter. It had taken the police two hours to get him out of his house. 'He keeps setting the alsatian on them. Man, it was a fucking riot,' said a Rasta.

Farissey listened with gathering impatience as the talk turned to the announcement that Madieson and Madieson Solicitors had taken up the brothers' defence. When someone pointed out that Victoria was joining the company, he shrugged. 'It's just a coincidence.'

An hour later, Victoria arrived at the Windsor. Farissey draped an arm around her shoulder. A Rasta passed him a long, crooked joint. He declined and whispered to the Rasta: 'It's all right; she's cool'. He watched as Victoria smoked tentatively, knew that, for her, it would be a pleasureless and isolating experience.

They moved from the balconies to the front bar through a connecting alleyway. At its opening, Farissey saw the friendless prostitute, the one the girls called Betty Boop, her fishnet legs wrapped in and out of each other. She was white-bloused and black-hotpanted, blowing soap bubbles under the lounge bar sign to invisible punters and river midges at the end of the block. She's not really a hustler, Lida had once told him. True enough: she's a schizophrenic.

Further along the alley, he saw a skinny white dealer telling a shaven-headed black guy that he had some 'top-notch Charlie'. Farissey remembered the press release made by Loudon Hargest on the day after the arrests. 'Butetown is an upside-down society,' he'd said. 'It is a place where violent crime and open drug-taking are commonplace, where people routinely wear knives as part of their clothing and where small fortunes are made by pimps and drug-dealers. A prime venue, in other words, for colonisation by Yardies.'

Upside down the area might be, Farissey granted. But small fortunes were not being made here. It was more like people scraping a living from bleak, challenging land, an abode of stones.

They joined Dolores and JD in the front bar. It was plush with deep-velvet furnishings; a time-scarred monument to older proprieties. Hatted and elderly black men sat bemoaning what had been gained, romancing all that was lost.

JD and Farissey consumed five or six units to Victoria's every one. Farissey was eager to please and entertain. 'My Dutch Uncle', he sometimes called JD, that or 'The Big Man'. At least fifteen people addressed the table with greetings, especially for Dolores.

Farissey saw Jess Simmonds enter the bar. He was wearing an oversized blue jumper with no shirt underneath. Jess nodded to the table and stationed himself at the other end of the bar. A few minutes later, Farissey joined him. Jess's blond mane was tied into a ponytail. He smiled a satyr-like smile whose secret was unknown, Farissey suspected, even to Jess himself.

Farissey listened with irritation as Jess outlined a plan to bring ecstasy down from Manchester and set up raves in the docks. 'The Bajas are inside and I need the money. Way things are heading, I'm gonna have to sell my guitars.'

Three years ago, Jess had inherited £25,000 on his father's death, the money being the first Jess had heard of him in twenty years. Farissey doubted there was more than two grand left of the inheritance.

'The culture won't travel down here,' said Farissey. 'The Idren'll move in. You end up with a baseball bat down your throat, they'll nick your gear and knock it out at their blues with the ganja and the sulphate and their horrible coke.'

'Are you in or not?' Jess asked.

'How many times, Jess? I'm not going to wreck a career on some half-arsed deal that'll go sour somewhere along the line.'

'Well, fuck you, Jack. After all these years.' Jess did his own faltering version of the hard stare. Farissey looked past him.

Victoria was staring at them with stoned, unsparing eyes. She saw them playing out the fiction of themselves. To those eyes, he and Jess might have seemed like allegorical figures. Where Jess was blond and hippieish, Farissey hid behind dark formality. But she wanted to see some truth behind their manifestations, some show of the bond or ghostly transaction that linked them. She wasn't looking at one or another but at a single mind that revealed its light and its dark aspects without the glimpse of a system, a symmetry.

Farissey retreated from that gaze. 'A word outside,' he said to Jess.

The alleyway was clear now but for a pariah dog at its opening.

'Let's forget about your business venture, Jess. For the moment, the thing is that Loudon Hargest *knows* we were involved in some way.'

'Hargest knows, I know,' Jess mocked. The band started up a version of the Stones's 'Ventilator Blues'. Jess whistled along contemptuously, found fault. 'Beauty of Keith Richards' rhythm guitar is the gaps he leaves.'

Farissey nodded. 'Admit it, Jess. You were thinking of setting me up.'

'Only playing around, Jack. I went along with the Bajas story after.'

'So what the fuck happened that night?'

'Be telling, that.' Jess resumed his whistling. He threw a stone at the dog. Still, the gangling mongrel stared down the alley.

'What you *don't* know is that Hargest put me under hypnosis. "Juicy stuff", he called it.'

Jess flung a fistful of stones at the dog. Arthritically, it loped off.

'What you say when you were hypnotised?' asked Jess, florid now, his features scrunched up.

'Be telling, that,' Farissey lied. He wished he did have something to withhold. Repeatedly he'd requested a tape or transcript of his hypnotic testimony. Last time he'd phoned, Hargest talked to him as though to a child. 'You're safe with me, Jack. No point in kicking up a fuss about that mumbo jumbo, is there?' A bluff? A card held close to Hargest's chest? A hostage to fortune? Farissey just could not know.

'All right, Jack. Let's trade.'

Jess drew breath, leaned back into the wall as he spoke. In the early hours of Easter Sunday, they had been smoking a joint in a narrow lane just along from the murder flat. Before they knew what had happened, someone bundled into them.

'You fell to the ground with him and you were sort of wrestling with him. I pulled him off and charged him against the wall – he was a weedy fucker. Anyway, blood starts spurting from his head, but he's not unconscious or anything. So I let him go.'

Jess didn't know how JD had found them. 'He tells me a girl's been stabbed to death. I had to shoulder you along the lanes to Windsor Esplanade. You weren't hurt, just out of it. JD wouldn't touch you because of the blood. Anyway, back at Windsor Esplanade, JD drives us to Sven Books.'

'So that guy was Mr X?'

'Certainly looks that way.'

'And we're going to witness against the Bajas *anyway*?'

Farissey waited for an answer, but Jess just shrugged, boxed up a conic joint. Farissey went to go back into the bar.

'Hang on,' Jess called. 'What about your hypnosis session?'

'Nothing more than a dreamy, fucked-up version of what you just said,' Farissey lied. Jess took a deep hit on the joint. Stymied now, his face livid.

'So that makes everything perfectly consistent,' Farissey prompted.

'Doesn't it just?' Jess's face was rigid, waxen, but a slight tremor spoke through his tones.

Next day, Farissey and Victoria paused at the Pier Head on their appointed Saturday afternoon walk. It was low tide, a gentle sunny fog on the water, the signal points obtruding like little cubist towers out of the mudflat. He pointed out a wading bird in the distance, how elegant it looked, how in tune with nature and its environment, and the seasons. How harmonious, how incurious, how unconcerned, above all.

'You know that colony is exceptional in Europe,' he said, speaking out his cigarette smoke with nervy relish. 'And then you get the Docklands Regeneration Corporation planning to make a barrage over it. When everything could be left just the way it is.'

He paused, straightened the knot in his silk tie. His voice shifted from its customary soft slurring to a kind of dry, metrical disdain, which she admired and detested, detested more of late. 'Do this, do that, do the other, when really there's no need to do anything at all.'

A rich and lyrical softness entered his voice as he spoke on. 'You know how things work here. See a guy coming at another guy with a bottle, a whore cursing out her pimp, see her pimp slap her – you just don't get fucking involved.'

'The trouble is,' she said, smiling to herself, 'if everyone thought like you, Jack, nothing would happen.' She cupped her hands against the breeze to light a cigarette. When did she learn to do that? Too late to ask such things, he supposed.

'Who's to say something's better than nothing?' He pondered his question and its futility vaguely, turned to look at the Pier Head Building, its castellated clock and hexagonal turrets announcing nothing whatever to the deadwater of the bay.

'Just suppose the Bajas didn't do it,' he continued. 'Then who did? Most likely some mother-obsessed pervert. And these people don't have records, they don't steal cars, deal drugs, assault police officers. They live in quiet little houses, drive quiet little cars and do quiet little jobs. Police haven't got a cat's chance in hell with them, and they know it. So why not pick up some real killers and have done with the whole damned thing? And it doesn't have to be retributive. Take them off the street, make things cosy for them. Plenty of cigarettes, Plato and por- nography: maybe even a few state-funded prostitute drops.'

'God, you can be a cynical bastard sometimes. Why not admit you're just so conservative?' She flicked her half-smoked ciga- rette over the rails.

'Because it doesn't need names like that. Think about it. Bajas in prison, Bajas free; a prostitute alive, a prostitute dead, the world at war, the world at peace, tide coming in, tide going out, one moon waxing, another moon waning, me alive, me dead, you thinking, me thinking – what fucking difference does it make?'

She didn't answer, at first. The breeze turned into a wind, whipped a ball of lugworms on to the breakwater. 'If that's the way you want it . . .'

Something spoke to him then. He looked at her, felt his body tense like a falcon before flight.

This is no place for justice, his look said. No place for dreams or ideals. Down here we console ourselves with the fact that we age a year at a time, and nothing else changes, nothing gets worse.

That evening they ate in the Red House, a bar–restaurant on the Penarth flats. They sat at a window table, watched the day disappear into the deepest blue. Farissey drank a bottle of wine during the meal. He picked at his food, left the vegetables untouched, commented on how good his mussels were, talked about the dangers of food poisoning during pregnancy. He became solicitous about vitamins, proteins and iron in her diet.

Meal over, he drank a run of Irish coffees. 'I suppose I should be supportive,' he said. The defence would need alibi witnesses – so much she knew – and access to Butetown's night world. Between running the pharmacy and spending his nights in the bars, he could help. 'I know just about everyone here. They might not like me, but they think of me as one of their own. And their mums and dads all knew my parents from the days they kept the House of Blazes. I've got their trust.'

'Keep an eye on me, in other words? My mother carries on like nothing ever happened. Oh, you're pregnant, *you* say. It's a bad business, JD says. But, oh my, it's no place for a girl like you, Auntie Dolores says. I listen to this and think what have they all got to hide?'

'Find, more like,' he muttered. He looked through the restaurant window. Heavy coastal darkness had gathered around the bay. He looked for a sign. Nothing out there but the odd, thin strips of lights from ships, a little moonglade; a world composed in all its amorality, a world with no truth to surrender.

They went to bed at two in the morning. As he dozed, images assailed him: *a clownish dwarf on a staircase vomiting minestrone into a soup bowl; a scarecrow shaking blood from its coat; a man lying on a floor beside a sprawled, blood-drenched woman; stroking her hair, whispering 'You don't fuck, you don't fuck' into her ear. A scarecrow appearing from nowhere onto Angelina Street like a shock into the night. Laughter, muted then shrieking, laughing mouths that disgorged police sirens; himself running from mirth, madness, chaos.* Then he was further away in time. *He and Jess, imprecisely younger, wandering miles and miles of meshed night, sitting on the Mardy Road rubbish tip, a tracking guilt at heel . . . he and Jess swaying eastwards past steel shutters and stone abandonment . . . he and Jess shoulder to shoulder, stumbling into whatever it was that they fled.*

He awoke at dawn. The early light curled around the bedroom curtains like long, thin, cruel fingers. Outside, the seagulls cawed like so many damned souls into Sunday's hush. Their messages flattened out into a dull rhythm in his head, merged with a discordant guitar piece Jess had composed many years ago. Jess came to mind; overcoated, poised, implacable: a vulture atop a clothes cupboard. The cawing moved up a tone. Nestled within its tendrils, its algebra, he heard: 'You don't fuck; you don't fuck; you don't fuck': heard it over and over like a litany, a chant, a mantra's refusal of time.

He tried to get back to sleep. When finally drowsy, he thought of water, secret water, the absolutely still water in that enclosed dock they call Dead Man's Point.

Then he remembered a story his father had told him about a crew of Madagascan seamen who'd sailed steadily on seemingly calm straits. Mile after mile they had been borne on an imperceptibly rising wave, not knowing the vast, watery ridge until it was too late.

Chapter Seven

For the next fortnight, Farissey kept a close eye on Victoria's work engagements. Her first task in the community was to interview Lida Varaillon on 14 May.

After work that day, Farissey walked to Lida's council house. He walked through a glorious evening, the air swelling with mid-May expectancy.

Lida was still asleep, Josie Marshall told him. She brought him into the front room. Josie was a muscular black woman in her late twenties. She had cropped hair and intelligent, sharp eyes. She was Lida's live-in lover. Technically, this made her Lida's pimp, but the reality, as Farissey knew, was that as housekeeper, childminder, mother to Lida's baby boy, Josie was the only person with any chance of holding Lida's life together.

'If your girlfriend's on the game like Lida is, you've got to put up with some shit, I knows that,' Josie said. 'But sharing a bed with someone who stinks like a fishpot in the bastard sun – that's more than I can take.'

Farissey half-listened, sipped on a can of Breaker, looked at the pretty black boy of about three months on the sofa opposite. He was quiet, contemplative, pumped out his arms and legs.

The room was spotlessly clean. Training weights were neatly stacked in the corner of the room. The early-evening news came on the television. Josie turned up the sound.

'Now little Daryl here, he's clean,' Josie said. 'Clean as a baby can be. It's me washes him. So why can't Lida wash herself? And what the fuck is she doing going out with no condoms? Eight o'clock in the morning she comes to bed today. Six in the evening now and she's only just getting up. What would happen to the little man if I waddn't around?'

'She's depressed, I suppose.'

'I knows that, Jack. I knows. But what am I going to do with that one?' Josie looked older, wiser and kinder now.

Farissey handed over a bottle of valium. 'This might help.'

'Thanks, Jack. Really. Thanks.' Josie put the valium on top of the television, lit a cigarette. She crouched on the floor, gazed remotely at the screen.

Josie had grown up in the white, working-class sticks. Grew up knowing she wasn't like the other girls, didn't like the clothes or music they liked, the talk they talked. But she was handy enough with her fists as girls go, handy enough to hold her own on the Bob Bank and to get into the hard core of Cardiff city's hooligan army. Then a friend put her on to the Butetown scene.

Down here, she'd found herself. Found she wasn't odd because she was black, wanted girls. And girls, pretty girls, were easy to get. A lot of the hustlers preferred going home to women at night. Trouble was, the hustlers weren't so much lesbian as battered down by bad men to about fifty–fifty. They played the boys off against the girls, the girls against the boys in a way that both beguiled and infuriated the sounder, more loyal sensibilities of Josie and her kind.

Lida slacked into the living room. She was wearing a white T-shirt, a black miniskirt and black suspenders. She looked agitated as she put her dark-brown hair up into a ponytail. 'I've made up a bottle for later,' she said.

'What you want – a fucking medal?' Josie turned her back, went upstairs.

Lida didn't react. She daubed some foundation on a large

bruise. 'Had an altercation with a pavement,' she said to Farissey.

Farissey witnessed the ritual that Josie must see daily before Lida took her stand at the dusk station. Open a Special Brew, roll a packed spliff ineptly, suck swig, suck swig, take up the baby as much out of desperation as love, cling to it as though the baby was shielding her from the world. Another Special Brew, a run of cigarettes. And suck swig, swig suck, put the child on the bottle the punters paid for. A couple of pork pies out of the fridge, toss off another can.

'Thanks for the valium, Jack,' Lida said, passing him a Special Brew. 'And for sitting in on that hypno thing.'

'You can pay me back in one,' he said. In a whisper, he told her that Victoria would be popping into the Custom House tonight. He'd be grateful if Lida didn't mention anything about the police interviewing him, JD or Jess.

'She'll find out in her own sweet time.'

'Sure. But I need the time to think.'

'You and me both. Course I won't say nothing, except what a fucking pain she is.'

'Easy does it, though . . . Can I meet you later?'

'S'pose so. Last orders in the Custom House?'

He drained his can with some relief. He was on his feet to leave when Josie came downstairs.

'What time you coming back?' Josie asked.

'Might be a bit late.'

'Lida, why's you going to be late again?'

Lida didn't respond. Josie took the baby, shouldered him. She looked more comfortable with little Daryl back in her arms. Strangers thought the baby was Josie's: black dad, white mother, just like Josie herself.

Lida stood in the middle of the room, trance-like in some goading silence.

'Why?' Josie asked again.

Finally Lida mouthed the words: 'This is why.'

'Yeah – off with some fucking bloke. Some fucking brother or another. Like Tony Baja was before you stitches him. And who were you with last night? There's no fucking business at five, six in the morning. And who's looking after the kid? Me again. Fucking muggins here. While you fucks those that pays you and then fucks those you pays.'

'Who fucking pays for everything round here? The punters pays, I pays.' Lida spoke softly.

'A tenner here, a fucking tenner there,' Josie said. 'There wouldn't be no food in the fridge if it waddn't for me.'

'Who needs feeding round here? The baby. Full fucking stop.'

'Why you going to be late? You never answers me, Lida.'

'When I finishes, I'm going down the North Star to spend some money, Josie. Spend as much as I can. All right?'

'Fucking fine. But if I hears you're off with any of the boys, I'll kill you,' Josie says at the door, as Lida steps into the gloomy cul-de-sac facing on to the murder flat.

'Then someone kills you, Josie.'

Lida's eyes mist over with tears. Knowing that Lida doesn't cry but just that once, and knowing that Lida thinks no one loves her enough to punch someone out for, Josie backs off, but not before Lida says: 'Like they kill Christina.'

That night Lida did three Pakistanis, one after the other, half a dozen jobs with regulars, mainly in cars, and then a couple of Arab guys who make her come to Les Croupiers casino — they give her tens and twenties in chips. She plays roulette while they go at the craps. She covers red and black both and cashes in a break even £200 this way, all the while gorging on the complimentary sandwiches and milky coffee. In the car park beside Aspro Travel Agents, one of the Arabs fucks her up the arse while the other watches and wanks. She picks up another £40.

At last orders in the Custom House, she tells Farissey it was her best and easiest night's work in months.

She sat beside him at the far end of the bar, a can of K in her hand and a cigarette dangling limply from fingers that are virtually manacled in tawdry rings.

Farissey soaked up the gloomy and watchful desperation of

the Custom House. Maybe a dozen people spread around, the jukebox playing the B-52s' 'Love Shack', four country-and-western lesbians at the pool table, a couple of grogblossomed dossers slumped back, the one hollering, the other asleep in a well-tailored brown jacket.

'Why the rings?'

'I wears them when I'm working. I always holds my keys in my hand, too. Only fucking precautions I'm taking these days.'

'How did that interview thing go?'

'Oh, it was fuck all, that. Your missus comes up and says "Sorry for the intrusion" and I tells her not to be sorry and just to fuck off because I've told everything to the police and a nice lady like whoever she is shouldn't have no fucking business in this place. Mind, you could've told me she was up the spout.'

A spasm went through Farissey's arm. His cigarette spun out of his hand. He retrieved it from the floor.

'How the fuck did that come up?'

'One of the girls started pushing her a bit. Wasn't nothing, pure front, you know. But that piece of yours, she must have taken it for real, 'cause she says: "Don't. I'm pregnant." A few of them thought she made it up 'cause she was bricking it, but she didn't look like the lying type to me.'

'She isn't.'

'Said she didn't know who the father was. Like that's some kind of deal. We all laughed. "That's a fucking first," I says to her.'

The well-tailored dosser woke up, turned in his chair. He coughed. Spaghetti-like lines of emphysemic vomit trailed onto his lapel. He rubbed it into the fabric, swilled his drink to its heeltaps.

'What's she going to do next?' Lida asked. 'Her family's all right, like, but this one hasn't got a hope. Don't know the score. The girls thought she was fucking social services. Asks me what man hit me to give me such a fucking bruise and I say it wasn't no fucking man.'

'The next one's different. She's going into the prison to interview the Bajas.'

By the look on Lida's face, he knew he shouldn't have said that. Something deeper than fear or betrayal flashed across her eyes.

'Someone said Carl's going to kill my baby when he gets out.' She looked down, drew circles in spilled beer on the counter.

'Who says Carl says? Anyone can spread crazy talk like that.'

'What the fuck am I going to do, Jack?'

'Ask Hargest for some protection. Then, you're going to forget about it, I suppose. Like a bad dream.'

'Sometime we'll have a good talk,' she said, now drawing smiling faces in the spilled beer.

Sometime we will, Farissey thought when she headed off to the North Star. He talked the barman into a few after-hours drinks. At one in the morning he left for his flat. He noticed the living-room light was still on. He turned into Angelina Street, smoked a cigarette, tried to compose himself. The bookies above the murder flat had started trading again. He pondered what Lida had said. Would Carl Baja kill a baby? No. But, then, whoever killed Christina killed her baby, too, albeit in its foetal form. He thought of the child inside Victoria, inching along the strand of its sex, its coat of genetic addresses already woven. When born, would he look for Jess in its eyes? Victoria was three months gone now; her scan was only ten days away. His stomach turned over. A scan made the idea tangible; features forming, the whole body growing, knocking on the door, trying to get into life.

Forget about it like a bad dream. He smiled sullenly, knew the hypocrisy of his counsel to Lida. Trying to forget, when they all needed to dream the bad dream again, wake bolt upright, a notebook or tape recorder at hand, a Loudon Hargest bedside; prompting, taking notes from that deep part of a soul, that core of a being you can't stick a knife into, that place where nothing mutates, nothing vanishes, nothing is lost.

He entered the flat quietly. Victoria was still up. She sat before a sandwich cut into eight tiny pieces. Two packets of chocolate bars were folded so very neatly on the side of the plate. It reminded him of his mother; a woman grown old beside her radio, eating currant cake for long-lost, girlish days.

The heirloom necklace in Victoria's lap was torn. It was her grandmother's necklace – all she or Dolores had left of that Trinidadian woman who arrived in Cardiff in 1936 only to entwine her destiny with a braggard refugee from the Spanish Civil War.

Farissey opened a bottle of wine in the kitchen. The curtains filled with light. Peering through the curtains, he saw it came from a searchlight over on the Dumballs Road.

'You could have taken me up on my offer. I could have been with you earlier on.'

'You heard?' She fiddled with the necklace. 'About saying I was pregnant too?'

'I heard.'

'You think Jess'll hear about it?'

'Probably. We'll have to tell everyone anyway. Can't have Dolores and your mum finding out second-hand.'

'I wasn't thinking. It just came out.'

'You did the right thing. Think about it: you could have lost the baby in there.'

'OK. I feel stupid enough as it is.'

'Why don't Madieson and Madieson send someone else in with you?'

'They would if I asked, but it's not the impression I want to create. There's always Thursday though . . .'

Farissey braced himself. That meant meeting Carl Baja again, one of only two men he dreaded.

'Count me in, then,' he said, at length.

At 3 a.m., Victoria awoke from a nightmare. In the dream, she was running through the corridors of a symmetrical house. Panicked, she tripped down an endless spiral staircase. She emerged in a deep tube station. There was some unspecified tragedy she had to avert. She recognised the station as the Angel. She pressed a button for a lift. The doors burst wide. Inside, she saw a small shape with a head of stars and clumpy feet. She picked it up. It was weightless, bandaged or swaddled. She lost hold of the bundle. It was scooped up and swirled into the tunnel as a train's cold air swept along the deep channels of the station.

Farissey spoke against the silence, the clammy, clawing dark. 'It's like the vision of Nebuchadnezzar. He saw a head of gold and clay feet.' A priest had once told Farissey that the stone which smashed the image was the one on which Jacob slept when he dreamed of his ladder to the stars.

'It's an abortion dream,' she said flatly. He turned on the bedside light. She was sitting upright in bed, her bare shoulders smooth to his touch.

'When I was up in London, the Angel was my tube. I remember just staying on the platform before going back to that student flat to tell a load of lies to everyone.'

'Maybe you've started dreaming about it because the guilt has lifted.'

'After the abortion, I just lay around with one question in my mind. I kept asking: How can you mourn for something you've never known?'

Farissey folded his arms behind his head. Something he'd never known beyond mourning for an innocence, for something always missing in him, a serenity he'd never possessed.

'You could always pray to Macha.' Farissey explained that in his father's Ireland, Macha was the patron saint of stillborn, miscarried and aborted foetuses. A cillineach was the place set aside for the repose of those tenuous, unfated souls.

'Like a cemetery?'

'Yeah, except that the cillineach is always hidden away, behind hedges on dead old tracks no one uses. And the ground is unconsecrated. I don't think anyone really goes there – you don't get a plot or headstone or anything. Besides, there are no names.'

He noticed that her hands were shaking under the bedcovers. He put his two hands over hers, gently at first and then harder, sluicing the tension out through her fingertips.

'Don't talk,' Farissey said. 'What does Billie Holiday say?

"Don't explain." Let's just smoke a few joints and laugh and cry and laugh and cry until we can sleep.'

She just wanted to be held. He did so until she was dead asleep. When the alarm went off at 7.45, he awoke with an image before his mind of Jess as a harlequin.

He was still holding her, softer than ever to his touch.

Thursday morning, they were in an interviewing room in Cardiff Jail. Farissey was struck again by the sheer hulking, thin-bearded, thin-moustached menace that was Carl Baja. He'd put on a good stone in weight since his incarceration but looked still stronger, handsomer and more assured. Carl pulled out a chair for Victoria. The prison officer left the room but didn't close the door. Tony Baja shook her hand with vigour. He was thinner, quicker, beset by stray energies, where Carl was all economy, containment. The Bajas slipped effortlessly into the small chairs and then into near-Buddhic stillness.

An aura surrounded these giants as if they were in possession of a common intuition or telepathy so vivid that it burst its channel and caught Farissey in its own dense and malevolent air. Without even changing expression, Tony communicated intensely to Farissey that Victoria wasn't a bad bit of off-white arse, and that he'd fuck it even on the outside, but also that he was sharp enough to manipulate any possibility to his advantage, however distantly it might be incarnated in this girl who didn't know shit from shit, but might just be eager enough to start a few ripples in those places where things can change.

Farissey pushed two hundred cigarettes across the table.

Carl gathered up all ten Benson & Hedges packets. A faint smile played across a face that seemed to have been carved from marble. A duty executed, his smile said, rather than a gift proffered.

'Long way from the school playground,' said Farissey.

'More like being back there,' replied Tony Baja.

'It's good someone listens to us,' said Carl. His voice was thick and low. 'We're true.'

He joined the tips of his fingers and thumbs, drawing his hands underneath his chin like a pagoda. All attention. All eyes.

'People say you had a grudge against Christina,' Victoria started.

'Sure we were a little upset with that prostitute, weren't we, Tony? Didn't show for that half-arsed shooting trial. But it was going back to court and she was supposed to testify *for* us. You don't see too many corpses in the witness stand, do you?'

'True,' she smiled in guarded appreciation, not sure if a joke or threat was intended. 'It doesn't make a lot of sense to get rid of *your* witnesses. But it's a connection, and once men with your sort of reputations are connected . . .'

'What reputations?' Tony Baja asked, his voice tuning up like the B string of a guitar.

'The police say that you are the first and second in command of a group called Inited Idren,' Victoria said, consulting her notes. 'They claim that the organisation runs prostitutes, deals drugs, possesses firearms, enforces debts and extorts protection money.'

'That's all talk. Cheap talk,' Carl said, chewing on his cigarette, determined to drain it of every last chemical. 'We don't have nothing to do with prostitutes.'

'There's no arguing about the firearms, though,' retorted Victoria. 'Glastonbury Festival, 1984. You went around all the hippie dealers, put sawn-off shotguns in their faces, stole their drugs and sold them on for thousands.'

'That was a little one-off,' Carl said. 'See, I hear they're selling drugs to kids just thirteen, fourteen. I got two little ones myself. I don't want them exposed when they gets older. Like I says in court, we were only doing the work that the police should've been doing.'

'How about the Yardie connections?'

'Our family came over from St Lucia. Yard men are from Jamaica. When they goes back, they goes "yard". Sure, I sees a few sometimes when I goes up to Birmingham to do some security work. That's all.'

Tony then took up the talk, explaining how it was a huge leap from selling a few drugs and moving competition off your turf to the kind of killing that some creep works on Christina. Farissey noted the way they worked. When one talked, the other kept his eyes firmly on her, scrutinising for any giveaways. They waited, watched, alternated. Just when they seemed to be losing interest, winding down, foreclosing her questions, the Bajas were rewarded with a revelation when Tony absently mentioned that half of Acram's pool team were drinking in the Avondale on the night of Easter Saturday.

'We needed to get some help for clearing up the Casablanca. So I pops round the Avondale. None of our boys was in, but there was about five of the Acram's players. That guy with the thalidomide who uses his toes as a bridge, and that pool hustler, Jimmy the Hat – great player, but a twat. They're all off their heads. That guitarist with the blond hair and ponytail, he was on one. More than E. Dust or some wicked shit. You knows him, Carl.'

'Yeah. Jess is his name,' Carl Baja says, some venality playing around his mouth and eyes, whether recalled or projected Farissey couldn't tell.

'Was anyone else on Angelina Street that night?'

'Plenty,' Carl Baja says, some enthusiasm in his voice now. Then he paused: quizzical, angry. He shifted his bulk in the chair.

'Wait a minute, spar, what the fuck is this? You was there, Jack. You tell her. You're both taking the fucking piss.'

Farissey shrugged, all eyes on him now. Good eyes, bad eyes; eyes alike burning with betrayal.

Sensing that they were on to something, Tony Baja took up the talk now, identifying JD as being present along with 'that fortune-teller woman'.

'You knows who I mean, Carl. Half-black, the one all the older guys used to get involved with. Too old for us, you know. Any case, we're picky.'

'Dolores?' Farissey yielded. They knew well enough, and enough to humiliate Victoria into naming her aunt in this context.

'Yeah, that's her,' Tony said, going on to describe a few of the pieces of trash that were hanging around for whatever reason, while Farissey bore witness, on Victoria's face, angular, attractive, and ever more mask-like, to a cyclical play of shock, anger, resistance and resolution that at once spoke of nobility and a child's fierce denunciation, of a complex of fears that could so easily be dispersed by a smile on the other's face, a small act of compassion or the simple words of exoneration that at least three of the four in that windowless and surprisingly dusty room longed above all to hear.

Chapter Eight

A week Saturday, Farissey saw Jess waiting by the embankment railings. Clever enough: catch him on Saturday lunchtime
when his nerves were in shreds. Nothing to do but receive Jess
with guarded courtesies. Farissey approached this figure like an
overgrown sprite leaning against the embankment railings. He
was dressed in biker's leathers. Did he always have to look so
cocksure, even on this Victorian terrace with the muddy, lifeless
Taff behind him, like one of hell's riders in this ruined place of
winds?

'Playing a gig at the Hoskins Club tonight. Want to come
along, blackjack? Black Jack Farissey?'

'Hoskins Club . . . I'll see.'

'Free pass on the door,' Jess grinned. He flicked his hair from
his eyes, a gesture Farissey remembered from his teenage years.
His mind backtracked a quarter-century, saw Jess in his gentle
and willowy adolescence. A bit hulkish now, though carrying it
well. But something gone from Jess, dead now, permanently
dead. Disappointed life of a dreamer who lets the years go by
without building on something. Ends up a heart-mystic, seen-it-
all, been-it-all druggie, motorcycle courier and roadie to

second-rate bands and theatre groups. A little kudos but without class, a song of blond hair on his head, a little breeze of a being unthreatening at first to young women because always in flight, fleeting like a sun-shot cloud and always onwards, into the other and making of their eyes his pools of exile. Not unlike Farissey would have been had sex been his first drug, had he played out his longing as a succession of easy beauties shifting with tide and season, scarce to be remembered but always acted upon until the reflection began to question, to speak.

'You given any thought to coming in on that deal?'

'I'm doing all right as I am.' Farissey's hangover had him feeling numb in the head, mouth and hands. His mind was racing: too many thoughts, no organising centre.

'Selling out, in other words. Isn't that what you're saying?'

'We're all selling out, Jess. You've got contacts, I've got contacts. You're knocking out street drugs, I'm knocking out legal drugs.'

'All right, Jack. Let's get back to where we are,' Jess said, turning away towards the River Taff, recomposing himself like a boxer between rounds. 'How things going with you?'

'Me? I'm just standing here with a bad head wondering why the fuck you stayed around here when I gave you everything you needed for Manchester.'

'I was commanded to stay here.'

'Subpoenaed?'

Jess braced himself, the old familiar anger escalating as he spoke. 'Don't get smart, Jack. Victoria got in touch. She was upset with you. She needed consoling, so I consoled her. Around Valentine's Day the little thing was conceived, wasn't it, Jack? Two Valentines. I did a little calculation about dates and figured I'm morally bound to take an interest in all this.'

Farissey lit a cigarette and crouched down with his back to the railings. In his oversized linen suit, he looked like a great implacable insect. The old dearth crept over him again, his chest tightening, knots in his stomach like the dry retches of withdrawal. He remembered Lida Varaillon slumped over a bar one night, pulling rings on and off her fingers. 'Mother's one, father's nothing,' she'd told him.

'Hang on a minute, hang on,' Farissey says, realising that he's losing the whole exchange, that this deadly game has spun off in directions he couldn't have foreseen. 'You mean you're actually claiming responsibility for the child?'

'For sure – it's the time. The time of life.' Jess slouched back against the railings. A coronation of river flies was forming around his head and neck.

'What're you going to do then, Jess? Set up blood tests, analyses of semen, court hearings, gather witnesses? Don't you think there's enough of that kind of thing going on round here as it is? And then you'll do for her what I can't do? Give me a break, Jess. You *hate* women, and you hate them most when you pretend to love them.' Farissey saw a razorbill, carried pontifically in the froth, the wash. He returned Jess's piercing, aquamarine stare.

'What you saying, Jack?'

'You know what I'm saying,' Farissey said, drawing deep on his cigarette. The smoke, concocted with adrenalin, made his lungs feel like a wide and dangerous valley. Power and dread in his chest. 'You say you remember that Saturday night? Maybe, but I remember earlier that day. I remember who you were arguing with, and it wasn't Vicky and it wasn't anybody we could ask about it now.'

He saw Jess withdraw, back down, back off. Neither one could force the other into such a corner of desperation that disclosure was the only way out. Farissey continued anyway, like a pool player sweeping his opponent's balls off the table when the game has been won.

'You know that defence is preparing pretty well, Jess. I'll bet the boys'll walk. They'll be back on these streets, and then it's anybody's guess where they'll choose to exact revenge.'

Farissey spent the afternoon drinking alone in the Packet. Five days ago, Victoria had gone out wearing a suede jacket and short black skirt – the very skirt that Jess used to suggest for those outings. Between themselves, Jess had told him, they'd elaborated a little theatre of passion which consisted of holding off orgasms much as small children postpone defecation for warming pleasures until the urgency of release overtakes the game.

Beginning with embraces, kissing, undressing, massage, Jess would guide her hands between her legs and caress her nipples as she slowly built herself up to a point as near orgasm as was possible. He would then pull her hand from her crotch and press down her thighs firmly so as to watch the undulations taper off as her body clawed its way back to rest. They would then re-dress, smoke a cigarette, make some tea, only to play out the same scene once again though with a deeper delirium, a greater compression and stronger arc of desire. Or they would just sit there, naked, looking at each other, until she could see the vivid aquamarine of his eyes in the rich sepia of hers, sitting there just at fingertip point, in reach and out of grasp.

They would go walking, shopping or board a circle bus to impose external frames on this tantalisation. Sitting upstairs on the bus, towards the back, Jess with his hand between her legs, kneading her clitoris slowly, staggering desire in concert with the stops, starts and stalls of the carriage. Passengers sensed what was happening, not from any visible clues, but from the heavy, insulating aura that surrounded them.

The journey completed, they would return to Jess's Atlantic Wharf flat. The rites of undressing and re-dressing would be repeated until the point when he could not but enter her; and he ever did so slowly, running his fingers from the nape of Victoria's neck to the opening of her buttocks, bringing himself in and out of her until this long ritual would issue in a starfall, a shock of rare colours, images of sun splintering through trees, or underwater grottoes. Later on, when the world had lost its light, they would drink and toke themselves into another form of ritual madness.

*

Farissey checked his train of thought, ordered a pint of SA and gave himself over to the Packet's ornate mirror. He asked a question of the mirror, of some deep recess within himself. What was the other hold Jess had over Victoria? The hold that was stronger than mere carnality? Had Jess told her the 'truth' of that night on Angelina Street? Or was it something to do with the baby? Or something else altogether? Some pact or subtle blackmailing? An image of Victoria's pregnancy scan came to mind: that small, incomprehensible bundle, curled on itself, waiting to unfurl, to find its form and features. Absently, he raised his pint of SA to his lips. Intense sunlight drew out its ambers. He thought of the Virgin Birth, of how the Holy Spirit impregnated Our Lady like sunlight which passes through a window without breaking it.

'You know I can feel your pain,' Victoria said when Farissey returned from his lone drinking session around seven-thirty that evening. He stood apart from her, looked at himself in the mirror. He looked so down, almost defeated. His hair was getting long and greasy. It was mopped over his head – he'd have looked loutish but for the nice striation of grey that ran through his tousles like sunshine along a river. He saw himself in ten years' time with iron-grey hair and the flushed, scarred face of a disappointed smallholder.

'You can feel my pain?' he said, almost in a whisper, pouring himself a tumblerful of whisky in the kitchen and opening the curtains on to the high prospect. He could see the odd light from the riverside houses on the Taff's Grangetown side.

'Yes, I can, Jack. I can feel what you must be going through with all this. I know what Jess has been saying,' she said, joining him at the window. 'I'm being straight with you.'

Think of yourself as something gentle, as some warm sea that can't be hurt by anything solid or sharp. Those had been Jess's words, his instructions as she knelt on the floor of his flat waiting and wondering why on earth he was putting on a condom. Then he started and she started and she cried silently as if sucking her outpouring into herself, felt like she could murder, scratch and stab because she was being scratched and stabbed by this animal. Blood rising in Jess's face afterwards like veins running through a chicken breast as he held the condom tight at the base of his penis.

'It was horrible. I suppose I had to go back one more time to be sure,' she said softly, as much to herself as to Farissey. 'So, yes, I lied. But just once. How many lies are you telling? I don't know who or what I'm living with.'

As he spoke, a long slur entered his voice like a noon shadow. 'I just don't remember a thing that night. Nothing beyond about one in the morning, leaving the Avondale with Jess, and Jess raving on about how I have to help him front some fucking drug deal. What's more, do you know what Jess was doing the day when Christina got killed? And do you know who that fucked-up hippie cunt was with that Saturday? How many different drugs he had in him? Five at least, including shiploads of angel dust. And others I can't tell you about.'

'Hold on a minute, hold on,' she said angrily. 'It's all a bit systematic, isn't it, Jack? Very neat. All an alibi for you to keep running, keep drinking, keep brooding, keep out of this whole game in which you don't have that sense of total mastery you can't live without.'

'I'm not paranoid. And even if I was, it wouldn't mean that Jess wasn't crashing with Christina a couple of days before she got killed and that I didn't see him saying "No one fucks with me, cunt, no one fucks with me, you hear, cunt" to Christina in the corridors of the Packet that lunchtime.'

He held himself straight, held her gaze. Nor does it mean, her gaze told him, that you didn't dip into a bit of that dust or eat a few Es yourself, Jack, not knowing what in heaven's name you did later on. Something captured on film by that God you think holds a lens to your every move; a Stranger God, one who exists only to dignify your loneliness, to provide an audience for the solipsistic show in which you are at once actor, writer, director. Neither that you didn't lose yourself in some terrible mess, just as the film keeps running when there's no one in the theatre to play its audience, the writer slipping out of his script like the *deus absconditus* of your bleak prayers.

'I know Jess was with her,' Victoria said. 'He told me the last time I saw him. What *you* don't know is that he helped Christina pack up that afternoon. Gave her nearly £300 and put her on the 4.25 train to Paddington.'

'You say you can feel my pain. Stand against the wall, then, put your hands up in the air and say you can feel my pain. When I turn around, I want to see you with both hands in the air and I want you to say "You know I can feel your pain".'

She backed off. 'We made a deal, too,' she said softly, holding his gaze. 'Remember?'

'Tell me you can feel my pain! Put your hands up in the air and say you can feel my pain! C'mon.' His voice planed down now: a hiss between tightening teeth. 'If you can say it, you can do it, too, can feel it, too,' he said, rinsing whisky around his mouth.

'I didn't mean to patronise you, Jack.' She backed off against the wall in blank apprehension. Not drunkenness in his vision, but drink-fuelled insanity: maybe some immense tiredness. 'I was only trying to sympathise.'

'Well, don't sympathise. Empathise. Right now,' he says, advancing on her, prowling her, balletic yet stiff-limbed like a Sufi dancer.

'What do you want me to do?' Her voice smalled off so pathetically that he might have hugged her but that she was responding too well. There was too much of her in everything. She couldn't get out without taking herself out, too, like that mystic tide which having washed away all things would still have to erase itself.

'Put your fucking hands up against the wall and say you can feel my pain,' he said, whisking his spirit glass from the table and prowling around her, prostrate as she was against the wall, but defiant where she was fearful and neither flesh nor spirit for strip-search or crucifixion.

'Jack, Jack,' and tremulous, like a flower, her voice breaking and telling him he could love her but not until he'd seen the white spaces, those sick and stretching as marshlands light her soul with the same horror of space that haunted him; only when he saw the perfect image of his own desolation. And now face to face.

'Put your fucking—'

And she raised both arms. Her eyes rolled back in her head, then rolled back to him.

Something he'd seen must have chimed with his sickness because he then sits down, bids her do the same. He holds her captive to his talk the next hour, pouring drinks, berating himself and telling her she must leave him for her own sake. Just as he goes quiet, he picks up his glass and crushes it into his hand. The shards mash into his palm until blood drips on to his black trousers. He keeps mashing the splinters until Victoria prises his palms apart.

He submits like a confused child, the message being 'I'm so brave: I'm cool to the point of death' in a youth that he might have told or twice told but whose sole message – she knew – was simply and poignantly and selfishly to 'love me or watch me kill myself: all of you'. It was a contempt of death that was more a refusal to look it head-on. That refusal was running now with memories and regrets and confusion across a face showing not pain but mystic elevation as though something in this experience had restored him to unclouded vision, the light of heaven pooling under stairwells, mirrored and made lofty once again in his hazel, now translucent eyes.

An hour later he woke up in his reading chair. The bedroom door was shut against him. He hirpled into the kitchen, dug some benzedrine from the depths of the freezer. He broke open two capsules – enough to skim the top off the booze – snorted them off the table. He had just enough time, he figured, to make Jess's gig at the Hoskins Club. He sat back in the chair, drank another whisky against the speed rush. He remembered Jess's words early in his relationship with Victoria. *Let's mix it all in, Black Jack. Like cement into a bucket.* Then Victoria's questions came back to mind. Why did Jess pull off his condoms when he was coming? Logical enough. Farissey's mistake in telling Jess he was having unprotected sex. Why keep them on now she was pregnant? Easy: no reason to relinquish his seed when it had nothing to act on.

Jack?, he hears when he gets to the foot of the stairs. A stifled plea in her voice. He won't respond. He takes in the street air. A stand-off they had lived in: his drinking against her infidelity; him against Jess. Always watching each other like animals who have stalked and fled so long that neither knows who is the hunter and who the quarry.

The Hoskins Club lay on Dumballs Road, a houseless, hushed industrial abandonment of auto-shops and ball-bearing factories with rust-peppered machinery in their forecourts. Jess had put together an ad hoc three-piece called Sharkworld for the night. The band started with a salsa-style version of Tim Buckley's 'Move with Me', ambled into a series of popular rhythm and blues covers, upped the performance with a note-perfect rendition of Hendrix's 'Little Ivy'. 'Hear My Train A'Coming' was a mess, but Jess's attenuated version of 'Machine Gun' captured a shard or echo of Hendrix's mournful violence, his violent mourning.

Farissey had settled at a corner of the bar. Jess's sister, Sophie, sidled along to join him. She was a plump, punky woman of thirty-seven with bright-red hair and watery eyes.

After a string of failed relationships, Sophie had returned to her mother's care with the same air of sulky lassitude with which she'd repudiated it some eighteen years ago.

'Playing good tonight,' Sophie said.

There were some two hundred people crammed into the club. Among all the bodies, Jess picked out Farissey.

'Next one is dedicated to someone I've brought out especially,' Jess said.

He teased and jangled around the most delicate of rock-funk riffs. He strung it out to an unendurable point, its source tugging away all the time at some buried part of Farissey's mind.

'Said he was playing good,' Jess's sister shouted in his ear.

The verse started up: Lou Reed's 'Kicks'. After drink drugs, sex – what next? Killing for kicks. At what cost life comes, how cheaply taken.

'Got his adrenalin flowing?' retorted Farissey.

'What's happening with Victoria? My mum thinks she's going to meet her.'

'What's your mother want to meet Victoria for?'

'Been forking out all this money for driving lessons for Jess. She says you got to have a car when you got kids.'

'So that'll leave you and me thinking, Jack. We'll be out on the sidelines.'

Sophie arranged herself coyly around the corner of the bar.

'We nearly got a little thing going.'

'A long way around the corner. Back when we were youngsters.'

Next loop around, Jess mimicked Lou Reed's rising mania, added from his own. He sang like a man half-strangled, or one shouting from under the sea, sang of murder as the acme, the final figure in the soul's exhausted series.

'You know why I haven't had a kid myself?'

'Never met the right man?'

'You *don't* know, then.'

Jess followed with an original number, a gentle, jazzy thing called 'Magic Girl' on which Farissey had imposed a reticent lyric: *My girl's full of tricks/She's a ventriloquist/Throws her husband's voice outside the door/And that gets me going good/Gets me going like a good boy should.*

'You used to write some lyrics for him, didn't you?'

'That's right.' He'd stopped more than ten years ago. Rock music had begun to seem juvenile then. Jess gleaned his reasons: another repudiation, another breach.

Jess slipped into a couple of Cowboy Junkies' numbers and sleepwalked through standard fare like 'Sweet Home Alabama'. He finished with a Steely Dan cover. He repeated the looping chorus over and over until the whole club was joining in. The wheel turning – taking him back where? To that room in which the blood came so cheap?

People congratulated Jess outside the club. He carried his guitar along the dark, industrial road. Most of the congregation streamed towards the docks in search of more drink. When the crowd had dispersed, Jess invited Farissey back to his Atlantic Wharf flat.

His flat was on the thirteenth floor. Atlantic Wharf was a new complex built around the East Dock like a dismal copy of Canary Wharf. As Jess opened the door, he seemed to forget that Farissey was beside him. The rush of solitude was tangible on the air; the door closing at home, the one that allowed recollection to run alongside desire. When inside, Jess wanted the window.

Farissey once again surveyed the dreary and tired orderliness of Jess's flat, with its one rubber plant, the electric and acoustic guitars, the battered-looking mandolin, amplifiers, sound systems, the old bureau in the corner – some jading imitation of a secretaire – the one in which he kept his condoms and his drugs and his sheet music. In a cabinet, Jess had neatly arranged his drug cases. A hundred and twenty plectrums and picks made from diverse materials were displayed and labelled on another table (Jess claimed to be thirty short of the world's largest collection). Along the walls, more than a thousand singles were arranged in alphabetical order. The only disorder was the movement of the fish in the tropical fish tank. Jess claimed to have rescued the fish when his mother stopped working at the Bute-town Aquarium.

They alternated between clean sulphate and coke as they popped open bottles of Grolsch. Jess rambled on about how disappointed he was that Farissey had kept him in the dark. It was just how he'd felt when Farissey had gone north to study pharmacy. He felt like Farissey had sucked the soul out of him and then tossed him away. He felt like that now, felt it literally.

Jess talked of Victoria, of the baby. He invoked those South American societies where all the men who have had sex with a woman during the nine months of pregnancy are regarded as joint biological fathers. He knew also of the Canela of Brazil who believe that the baby will bear the features of the man who contributed the most sperm during the woman's confinement.

He spun out an impossible dream. He and Jack were somehow conjoined in this foetus. Their sperm had met the egg and merged in some inconceivable alchemy. It was a miracle child; Victoria was but the vessel, the occasion, the web in which the fruit hung.

'Half Simmonds; half Farissey. How about that?'

Jess went silent, picked up his unplugged guitar. His left hand moved along the fretboard with the thoughtless and wilful precision of a swift-moving tropical spider.

Everything's upside down in Jess's mind, Farissey thought. Now Jess was in the shadows; the very thing he would have run from had become a lure, a risk and a haven. The games with girls and mirrors weren't necessary for the moment. Jess didn't need to flee the self because he was full again with loss and the expectation of loss.

'Your wife, for fuck's sake. "Jack's girl".' He curled his lips around the word 'girl'. 'Girl' didn't have a fucking thing to do with it.

Jess went back to the window, looked over at a Butetown now alien, suspended between its day-self and its night-self. He talked to himself. Butetown can wait for a day or so, can't she? *She can*. Wait for Jess. Manchester, too. That bitch can wait a few weeks, can't she?

The window view told Jess how much clout he was soon to wield. Small fishing in Manchester would make him *someone* in his home town. Jess talked of the people of Butetown as though they were so many dying flies or colonies of termites inching towards extinction. A glimpse of the prison tower raised his mania further. The Bajas were there; he was here. Soon, half the town would be jumping through his hoops.

'The whole bay high on my drugs and it won't know where they're coming from.' It could all wait; wait for the day time, wait for Jess.

'Jack, man, we got to stay close. Close, like that.' He crossed his fingers beside his temple. The crossed fingers looked like a pincer.

Farissey left without saying goodbye. It was never part of

the ritual. Jess thought himself everywhere and everything. He mistook his loneliness for power: it could fill oceans, deserts.

Farissey took the lift down the thirteen floors to ground. Outside, white housing lights played on the dark, breeze-ruffled water. He felt Jess's eyes tracking him from above. It didn't matter. He wasn't free by any means, but he was moving.

The first lights of day were in the sky. He walked down the slow scree of the bay to the shoreline. He wanted to merge with the coming morning. He tiptoed into the flat, opened a bottle of chilled white wine, took it to the shoreline.

He thought back some ten or twelve years ago. Benares. He'd just returned to Cardiff after qualifying as a pharmacist. He wasn't in any rush to start working. He and Jess had gone to India with the intention of producing a pictorial history of Calcutta. Nothing came of it. Jess had to placate a girl's father by surrendering his camera. Then they got stranded in Benares, gazing out at the river and shooting up morphine beside cancered Brahmans. That was when he'd let Jess back into his life.

He knew now that he'd let a part of himself slide into Jess's mould again. It was a genuine part of himself, he knew. One that he'd taken arms against, for sure, but something that still called to his deepest nature.

He looked at the early-morning sunshine on the hills of Penarth, felt the warmth, felt the long, hot summer coming on. He sat, cross-legged, sipping the wine, looking at the estuary just as he'd looked at the river in Benares. He sat for maybe four hours, lost himself again in that dawn, felt less like a person than an echo, a run of frost on a lawn, a glimpse of winter sun on a reservoir. He lost himself somewhere between living and desisting, between inhabiting Jack Farissey and observing Jack Farissey. Between thinking and – in some deadly, dulling way – being thought.

Chapter Nine

For the rest of that Sunday morning, he sat in the flat drinking larger and larger measures of vodka. He couldn't drink himself down, took to the street, tried to walk the speedball out of his pores. As he walked, he longed for Monday, for work and its clarity. He headed up to town but it gave him no relief. Cardiff loomed over him. He looked at the Catholic cathedral in the distance. He thought of spires, telegraph poles and pylons: a viral horizon. Everything angular, exact, amoral, brooding with cold, calibrated intelligence.

Lunchtime, he bumped into Josie Marshall in Val's Bistro. She had the baby with her, joined his table. She was wearing a sweatshirt and shorts. He folded up his newspapers. She placed the baby on the table. Between the cutlery and condiments, it looked as though he were the dish of the day. Smoke circled around his head. She was edgy and distracted, something imploring in her look. On her second beer, she launched into a rambling account of how Lida had been arrested at dawn.

'Lida brings round a whole crew at half-six. Stereo cranked right up, drinking Special Brew, skinning up. Some fucking Sunday morning.'

'Can the police detain people for making too much noise?' asked Farissey.

'They say "breach of the peace" but that's not why they wants her. Say they've got the results of blood tests in the room where Tina got topped. And the tests don't fit with the Bajas. The coppers even start laying into me, then: some jealousy thing on account of Christina being Lida's best friend and *her* being *white* and *me* being paranoid about *her* being *white* and *me* being *black* – usual fucking police bollocks. Sure, Lida had a thing going with Tina, too – but that doesn't mean I go carving up the girl, does it? The police saw they was making cunts of themselves so that was the end of that.'

A dread gripped Farissey. Not for himself so much as for a being that can't or won't remember, a self that has lost that silver thread of memory, of continuity. He gazed down at his injured palm with its network of bloody lines, coagulated blood. What blood in that room . . .? His own? He wanted to remember, to be judged and to atone.

'How about Lida?'

'They've let her out already. She's drinking her face off in the Custom House. Can't look at things straight, that girl. This is now – what happens if the Bajas gets off? They knows who stitched them up.' Josie went silent, gathered the baby to herself with the watchful solemnity of an abductress.

'Suited you at the time, Josie. Suited all of us.'

'Lida's a coward,' Josie whispered. 'She's a lying bitch. If it waddn't for little Daryl here, I'd have fucked off ages ago.' She paused. 'Sorry, Jack. I didn't mean that you're a liar too.'

He smiled. 'No worries. I don't know if I'm a liar or not.'

'How about you? You gonna get dragged in by Hargest?'

'I doubt it. That's not the way he leans on me.'

It wouldn't be. Hargest rang the pharmacy the next day, mid-morning, with some menacing camaraderie in his tones. Business was slow for the remainder of the morning. Farissey sat in the back room of the pharmacy filling out documents for a government audit. He signed and dated a form, realised it was his father's twenty-fifth anniversary in a fortnight. Must get a Mass said, he thought. Just then, he was called into the front of the shop to talk to a Somali woman with a prescription for amoxycillin. Her son had quinsy. 'I think he should be in the hospital,' she said. 'Not even a teaspoon of water passes down his throat.'

Farissey told her to administer paracetamol plus double doses of the antibiotic on the first day. 'Take his temperature on the hour. If it comes down, he'll be on the mend. If not, ring your G.P. If you can't get a visit, give me a call.' He put his business card on the counter, circled the phone number, placed a thermometer amidst the paracetamol and antibiotic. She looked flustered. 'No money,' he said. 'It is your entitlement in this country.' He made a cryptic note to himself. He would balance this little irregularity from his own pocket.

It was one-fifteen when Hargest arrived at the flat. He settled in the reading chair, a light briefcase in his lap, arms folded across his chest, a sloppy grin on his face. He opened the briefcase, inspected its contents.

'Don't let me stop you having a drink, Jack.'

'You haven't.' Farissey shifted his vodka tumbler from hand to hand. He stared directly at Hargest, at his beady eyes, his pockmarked face. Hargest asked for whisky and water.

'I made sure your good lady wouldn't be around. She's with that Madieson and Madieson outfit at the station right now. Nosing around, causing trouble. Trouble for all of us, trouble for you, too, my son.'

Hargest settled back into the chair, sipped on his whisky. As he settled, an overripe dreariness came over that front room.

'I suppose you're a bit worried right now, thinking chances are the Baja brothers will get acquitted. Now, you're not sure if they'll learn that you played a part in getting them arrested. So you and I have a bit of common cause, you understand.'

'I understand,' resigned Farissey.

'Good.' Hargest leaned forwards. As he spoke, he waved his finger like a baton. 'Cities. Cities are full of men who want to

harm young women. Men about your age. And they like stabbing because it's full-on and in their scumbag minds it's a bit
like fucking, maybe more like fucking than fucking itself.'

Hargest got to his feet, shuffled across to the sound system.
Keys jangled on his belt, his broad hips.

'Mind if I play you something?'

'Not at all,' replied Farissey, staring down at his black
brogues.

A dreary monotone filled the room. Farissey's own voice, yet
flattened out, somehow unearthly, lacquered.

*'And at that moment she knew she'd never be a mother; she knew
that the only sacred and defended space that was for ever her own
would be hers no longer as he comes at her again looking as he did
and he's not himself, the strength, running up through his arms, it's
all electricity, his face, sweating, throbbing, so clinical as well, dear
God, so far gone she'd seen that look before but hadn't realised what
it meant until now, like he wanted to take her but then some and it's
all too much to bear losing blood as she was and she knew it was over
for good, and she's wondering too why'd she ever let him back, when
she felt something coming on like this, why she always drew the
worst, kept returning to it; the sound of cars in the background, there
was, then shouting, arguing, the usual hustles, deals or pimps and
hustlers, and she wished she was there in the thick of things, scared of
it as she was, all this hell to pay in the street, there was, and she
makes for the window, gets there long enough to see that it's blue, like
the streets and the sky were bruised: so cold, a scalpel nearly and
where'd he get it from? Hadn't seen anything when he comes in
and she wonders how it could be so bright out there, and she feels like
she's in a cage and wants to claw or scratch her way out, but she's
just pawing, velvet and sort of electric, and her head shocked like
light flooding along the canal – calm, eerie sheen – and he grasps her
hair and twists her around as he presses one hand hard into her face,
holding it with fingers, thin, so strong – that's when the cutting
starts, the pain hits, God above, from the inside out, a goose walking
over your grave, like nothing you'd ever feel, fingernails ripped, close
to the bone, whirling now, losing it, another world, all those loving
faces, this love, like drowning, her mother, lost, like her child could*

keep her, kind and helpless now, funny, how sticky, how warm, you wouldn't think – eyes stare out of puddles, she thinks he must be going for her groin but if he is he just keeps missing saying something, maybe sobbing, "Forgive me, I'm sorry, it's not you, it's not me" and she's running her eyes along the knife, the fingers, the hand, to a face, wet with tears, frozen in frenzy, pushing itself into trance, calling some other power to act. Would've been a girl, she thinks, she knows, the door burst wide at the very point of breath. "Have I lost you altogether, in this wrenching, in this blood? Have I lost you when I'm so full to bursting with the emptying of you?", like nothing on earth, not a word nor a picture to fit, a place begone, down the dark shafts driven. "Wasn't our little girl any more" – of a child dreamed, dreamed of that solely, what was that? taping or ticking silver thread shot through the flesh; couldn't look too long at – seeing – naked bulb, ashtray, unused but open condoms spotted or flecked ceiling blood of walls, hers, like it was fixed and nothing in that room would ever change again – wanting the blood? – that being the last he had of her, scarcely sheltered from a cold that seemed to come as much from inside as from that hoary room like he was wringing the blood from his hands, huddled for mercy on the floor, two hours in which to shift to another story never-ending where it never started, playing itself out infinitely, yes, to turn his own trick with this filth and take its returns.'

'That good enough for you, Jack?' Hargest replaced the tape in his briefcase. He gave Farissey a stapled, seven-page transcript of his hypnotherapy statement. The detective drew his attention to a handwritten comment on the covering page. *Of no significance as evidence. Subject is playing out an abortion fantasy?*

'You've always been safe with me,' Hargest said. 'And you'll stay that way so long as you do some thinking. In a few weeks time, I'll set up a meeting with you and JD in Kiwi's Bar. So you've got plenty of time to remember exactly where you were in that room, how the Baja brothers killed Christina Villers and how it all fits with what you said under hypnosis.

'Seek and ye shall find,' Hargest said at the door. Farissey looked down Bute Street as Hargest walked townward – grey jacket slung across his shoulder, shirt sweated to his back – like an image of bleak, avuncular corruption.

He went back into the pharmacy. He wrote a letter to Father Dennis Dunn of St Cuthbert's parish, enclosed a cheque for £50. *'Have you remembered your father's anniversary? Have you arranged for a Mass to be said?'* His mother's words in her demented years: words spoken out against the growing darkness of her mind. Words that would bid her to go to the drawer and press £20 into his hand. *'And are you still drinking?'* I am. *'And have you kept the faith? Do you still have the faith?'*

'Yes,' he would tell her. Empty as the skies might be, there were still countless caves and recesses in which God's shadow showed forth. But his faith wasn't her faith. It was a grim, nocturnal faith without which life could be no more than a brute journey enlivened by the brief releases of drugs and orgasm, the spectacles of cruelty and awe: here, today, the solitary wasteland of the killer.

He changed into a blue linen suit, white linen shirt, silk tie of subdued gold. He stepped on to Bute Street with no mission in mind. The evening was hot, presaged nothing of night. He walked slowly, stultified but strangely receptive. His soul was open to sights and feelings normally crowded out by work and preoccupation. He saw the beautiful cross of St Mary's next to the blank, Eastern-bloc front of the Salvation Army hostel. He thought of how the mass of suffering gathers. He wondered if the problem of evil enhanced as time moved on and new evil was added to old or whether each new evil brought the world closer to the end of evil. Perhaps time itself was evil, he speculated, but that begged the question as to why God made time in the first place.

He thought of the constant figure of betrayal that threaded through his recent dreams, wondered if dreams were not a foretaste of hell. In one dream, he was defending himself against a throng of Butetowners; outdoors, in a time-misted puritan court. Butetown faces tightened in rictuses, in accusation. A nocturnal girl hovered on the outskirts of the community, of the judges of Jack Farissey. She pointed the finger, her eyes blazing like pearls.

What were these dreams telling him? Nothing but that he had been in the room when Christina was killed. But who was the 'he' of whom his hypnotised self spoke? He thought of a secret self, a sharer: a darker self that read the self, saw its real motives. He recalled that self-improvement reading he'd done in his early twenties. *Othello* came first to mind. He had no trouble in seeing Iago as the shadow self of the Moor. Then, he thought of the witches who spoke to Macbeth of his darkest longings; of the Fool who mocks, chides and befuddles Lear with riddles of things past, passing and to come; next, of Hamlet, whose ghost father came back to redirect his son's almost blunted purpose.

Farissey paused, prayed for clarity, vision. What was this other which was also the self? He was rejoined by the image of a face, the face of any woman who sorrows alone. Dignity spoke through its well-sculpted, middle-aged features. The face was faraway, at the most remote point of seeing. He then saw an arid track opening on to a country lane and a long, desolate road that led over a hill and down to a sea that offered not peace but dissolution. He interpreted the vision to mean that there was no moral centre, no way of the good to follow.

At the Custom House, he saw Lida Varaillon. Her clothes were dirty. She was drunk, too drunk for the cars or their punters. She swigged on a bottle of beer. She cocked her hip out listlessly, looked upwards as though questioning the sky, its busy clouds. He wondered how much more the poor girl could take. A speech formed in his mind, a speech of consolation. He passed on, the words sounding dead in his head: rehearsed, like an oration or sermon.

There were times, he knew, when faith seemed little short of moronic; no more adequate than is a road atlas to a country, a child's sketch to sea, mountain and sky.

*

That night, he drank in the Custom House and fetched up in the North Star. He had cover for work the following day. Victoria was in a suburban restaurant with the defence team.

The North Star was the end of the Cardiff night even if – at 4 a.m. – it did close earlier than Val's Bistro, or the Cabbies' Club and King's Snooker up in town. Farissey was uncertain of his status there since Victoria's involvement in the Bajas' defence but figured he'd be OK if he kept stepping on the offbeat with the rest of them.

Come midnight, he was drinking whisky alongside ship guys silently bent over the bar with sweat-soaked and blinkered eyes. He relished the claustrophobia. The place was windowless and smelled of rat poison; draped and Bathesda-black. Lesbians and hustlers crowded around the tiny dancing area; two-bit dealers sat in the corners. He knew the North Star wouldn't go on much longer. No one saw themselves there in five years' turning. They were all marking time as a long-distance driver knocks down the miles with the minutes, not for landscape and prospect but to have done with journey and destination.

At one in the morning he settled with Jimmy the Hat for a half-gramme of coke. The two of them snorted lines off the counter. Jimmy the Hat talked about his progressive liver disease, about how he didn't want to live more than another five years. He wanted to end his days beside the Ganges, gazing on to the water, waiting and praying. To a fatalism such as Farissey's, which doubted that the future could be changed any more than the past, Jimmy was somehow already there, converted, at peace, dying in another world. He felt as though he and Jimmy were the only people left in the universe, aboard the train that leaves after the last train, in a hurtling carriage that had never departed and would never arrive.

Just as Farissey was about to line up some more coke, the DJ cut the music mid-track. Through the jostling, Farissey could see that a fight had broken out between Josie and Lida. Josie had Lida pinned – knees on chest – to the dance floor. She pounded Lida's face, then menaced her eyes with a lighted cigarette.

'Talk, you lying white bitch; talk, you fucking Tom Pepper, 'cause you knows, Lida, if anyone fucking knows.'

'I don't know, Josie; honest, I don't.'

'If you'd told the fucking truth we wouldn't be in this shit. And what you say instead of telling the truth? That they makes you poke a knife into Tina's guts. What did it feel like? Doing that to your best fucking friend?'

'Fucking stop it, Josie. Fucking stop it.'

And stop she did, and there was silence, a silence you could ignite as Josie gets off Lida and swaggers out in a wake of hurt and defiance.

The club clears effortlessly. No one even finishes their drinks. The barman announces that Josie's banned. Everyone disperses in the sure knowledge that a real transgression has taken place tonight in a bar where, with connections even less than Josie has, you could carry a body out, throw it into the Roath Basin and still be let back in for the last drink.

Farissey loses Jimmy the Hat in the mayhem. He lingers outside with the black dealers. No cops around, but everyone's still talking smoke under their breath.

Farissey is standing near Lida and Primo, a black dealer and her current lover. She has her soft brown–black hair in a pony-tail and is looking vulnerable and fierce at the same time as she leans against a lamppost. Tears have made Lida's mascara run down her face, fissured her make-up to reveal a series of old bruises beneath the reddening her face has taken from Josie. A punter, Farissey is told later. Primo hadn't wanted to take her to the North Star on account of everyone assuming it was him who knocked her about that bad.

'Everyone's at me, Primo. Everyone's fucking at me. I can't turn nowhere. I can't stand it,' she says, kicking the lamppost. 'Do something, do something for fuck's sake.' She pounds her fists on his chest, instinctively, like a suckling for its mother, not for malice but for want of language. 'Someone's got to do something. They're all after me. And no one loved Tina like I did. I gets all the grief and I gets all the fucking shit. Some-body's got to do something.'

Farissey followed her into the lemon and yellow haven of Val's Bistro. Lida was sitting alone. The bistro wasn't busy. A couple of skint druggies opposite were quarrelsomely sharing a plate of chips and a pint of cider.

He felt strangely at peace sitting across from this dark, willowy girl, as shy in body as she was in look. He remembered her before Christina's death, how she believed in having a good time regardless of the next day, the world's news, the week's laundry. He looked at the powder blue of her shirt, her face shocked pale now, and those huge, heavy red-lipsticked and ever-moist lips.

She snorted a line of his coke from the shelf beside the table. He could see it run up her being. They drank wine out of carafes as though it were beer. As the wine took hold, he rambled about longing for God but saw that what he sought was only a glimmer or reflection of himself. He felt as though he was looking at himself with her eyes now – Victoria's eyes, too – only to find that he wasn't any kind of thing at all in himself, just some dark shelter inflecting absence along registers, destinies and counters.

'What you want God for?' Lida asks, drawing breathily on a cigarette and flicking purple-tinted hair from her eyes. 'God don't make no fucking difference, and if he do then it's too late for the likes of me.

'I likes you, you're different,' she slacked on, 'but I don't know why you hang around.'

Gently, he rested a hand on hers, dragged on a cigarette from the other. She was right, in her way. Down here, there was nothing for him. Down here, he could play out his failures as a pageant, people as so many players entrained, so many ghostly witnesses to his failure to seek out his better self.

'You got everything. You got a good job, your missus is beautiful. Stick with what you got – you might even get to like it. You got a baby coming, too. And there's two of you. It in't easy when the father fucks off.'

And then she laughed as the wine got its grip on her too. Everything in her chimed when she laughed, despair sitting on her existence like a fool's cap and bells. She laughed as if to say

'What have I said? Me of all people?' and postboxered her lips around another glass, like a toad going down from its leaf to draw on the stagnant pond.

'How far gone is she anyway?'

'About fifteen weeks.'

'Boy or girl?'

'A girl. That's what the scan shows.' Again that hypnotised voice coiled around him: *Would've been a girl, she thinks, she knows, the door burst wide at the very point of breath.*

'You don't exactly look over the moon about it.'

'She isn't carrying this child for me, not even for herself. Something else wants it, the same brutal thing that keeps us all spawning and fighting and eating and complaining and dreaming up other worlds to shield ourselves from where we are.'

He lined up more coke on the shelf. 'Think about it from a man's point of view,' he said, rising on the coke, rising on his own rhetoric. 'You have all the anxiety about the birth, the crying, the nappies, the teething, the sleepless nights, the death of desire between father and mother – just like when a third person comes into the room – and the expense, and the schooling, and then the murderous, sulky adolescence when you become the image of everything the offspring loathes in itself, and then you have the slip of a daughter who gets pregnant, or the mad son who gets sent to prison, and then the divorce, and, as you shrivel and he or she grows, the new family shunts you off to an old people's home, puts up with you for dinner one Sunday a month – and after all that you don't know that the child was your own in the first place.'

Lida smiled. Farissey looked directly into her face. It was a smile before which a person could lapse, cease, submit like sands to the sea. 'What the fuck was all that in aid of?' she asked.

'I've got a really low sperm count. I had myself checked out, got the results a couple of days ago. My doctor says there's not a cat's chance in hell that I'm the father of that child.'

'I thought something was bothering you. Changes things,

that—' she fiddled around in her handbag looking for more cigarettes '—for the fucking worse.'

'How about Christina. Whose baby was she carrying?'

'Tony Baja's, maybe. I don't know.' She went silent for a while, dragged heavily on her cigarette, allowed her head to follow the slope of her shoulder, gave her eyes over to that waking sleep.

Some computeless clocktime on, she said: 'That missus of yours is causing a lot of fucking trouble – in all sorts of ways.'

'I know,' Farissey said. 'That's why we've got to get you out of Cardiff. The police have got to do something after what you did for them. I'll have a word with my friend, JD.'

'I'll think about it, when I'm straight, like.' She pulled herself up in her seat. 'There you go. I feels bigger and straighter now.'

He thought of Victoria trying to unravel a mystery whose solution was no further away than might be his companion's lips from another glass, lips that were saying to him, 'You know if Primo finds out you're with me he'll do you like he wouldn't one of the black guys', and he himself replying, with some attempt at humour, that it's Josie worries him most and that Primo can kill him, but won't find out and there won't be anything to find out because Farissey's here as a friend (and isn't Primo in the Idren?) and besides he could claim to be a punter for all Primo knows.

Perhaps he is, perhaps they both are: but Lida insists on paying the drinks bill, generous as she is anyway, but still to mark a difference.

Someone's got to do something, Farissey thought, as he crept into bed a couple of hours before Victoria's alarm would go off. He tried to sleep, but the coke was still on him, lustreless now, an irritation. A song was working around his mind. John Martyn's 'Solid Air'. What had he been doing? Taking his time, living on . . .

*

Someone's got to do something. But why him? Or who? Him? Jack Farissey? A name summoning him into being. Like a jackal calling. Letters to the blood-letting.

He spent most of the following day sipping vodka in bed. By seven o'clock he was bathed, showered and sitting with Dolores and JD at Windsor Esplanade. It was the last week of May.

The evening was balmy, hanging and breezeless. They sat in the back yard that JD formerly used for storing wheelbarrows and cement mixers. JD had laid a patio at Dolores's request. Exotic plants and dense foliage surrounded the plastic chairs and table on which lay white wine, orange juice, fruit and the remnants of a Caribbean meal. Tired cosmos daisies rose flutterlessly in front of bushes of purple-flowering Tibouchina. In the back lane, a few Asian boys and their dog were lamely following a football.

Dolores fetched into her handbag. She pulled out a photograph. It captured a family scene circa 1969: the dark, crude-featured father, the elegant mother, her hair flowing and natural, a baby held aloft between them.

'That's the sort of thing Victoria's bringing around. Thinks Christina's mother might still be alive.'

Farissey looked at the photograph. Christina's mother had a serious, melancholy expression; she was beautiful in a tranquil and abstracted manner. Her shoulder-length auburn hair framed high and sharp cheekbones. Her expression spoke of serene disaffection with the stocky, gap-toothed man whom she was soon to leave. The baby was held aloft between them. Nothing in those baby eyes: just the empty globes which looked back from the last photographs of her corpse. *Eyes stare out of puddles.* Where were these words coming from?

JD shifted his bulk in the bucket seat, bit the end from a fresh cigar. 'I lost a daughter, you both know that,' he said.

Five years ago. JD stopping off for a cup of tea between jobs. His daughter puts on the kettle, JD plays with his toddler grandchildren on the floor. Twenty-eight years old his daughter was, and struck down by a brain haemorrhage. Dead before she hit the ground. JD's first wife died of emphysema the following year.

'So what's Victoria planning to do?' JD asked. 'Track the mother down in her new life and say here's your daughter, except she's dead now? Or send the mother copies of the Polaroids, that it?'

'This is the corpse that was your daughter,' Farissey muttered absently.

'Christina wanted a baby,' interjected Dolores. 'Victoria should be grateful she's making something where that girl didn't have the chance. Like I told her, motherhood and murder – there's two things that don't go together.'

An argument started up in the back lane. Myriad small voices, a dog's exhausted barking. JD rose to his feet, his golf shirt riding over his paunch. He went into the back yard wall, said something like: 'What's the bother, lads?'

'What did the Bajas have to say for themselves?' asked Dolores as she fished the single ice cube out of her gin and tonic.

Farissey paused as she sucked on the ice. A tipless cigarette dangled from his lips as he vacillated between his glass of wine and the malt whisky JD had laid on the table.

'Just what you'd imagine. Me – I didn't tell Victoria anything.'

'God bless you, Jack,' Dolores trilled involuntarily through the sputum that normally gave her voice a grain of gravelling, bronchitic lore. 'If we're not very careful, all sorts of things will come out of this. Any direction you look in . . .'

'I think a few have already, Dolores.' He thought of the ghost that had flitted beside him a few hours ago: eyes alight with accusation, shyness and hurt.

'Victoria knows we were there that night,' Farissey said, repelling wasps from his drink. 'Jess and all. The Bajas told her the whole story.'

Dolores pushed her flock of hair back with four thin, perfectly sculpted and seemingly artificial fingers, fingers that seemed to be elaborating he didn't know what, cancers or cures.

'Told what?' she asked as JD distributed pound coins among the Asian kids. 'You told her a few stories. Like I used to tell the girl when she was a child to get her off to sleep. The way children get frightened in the night. She'll have to deal with all that soon. You too, Jack.'

Just before ten in the evening, Farissey walked back to the flat, enjoying the whisky buzz in a melancholy sort of way. A flaxen-haired girl was shouting through the letterbox. She was wearing a black T-shirt, grey leggings and stilettos.

'Fuck right off, mister,' she said as he approached.

'I own this place, love,' he said. Why she backed off, he didn't know. The reek of alcohol, something in his eyes.

'I want a morning-after pill. Except it's a night-after pill, see.' Acne blossomed across her forehead. She didn't have a woman's hips, looked scarcely a day over fourteen.

'You're supposed to go through your GP.'

'My GP ain't open. Nor's your chemist's shop, if you really owns it, like.'

Farissey pulled his keys from his pocket, dangled them in front of her face.

'Sorry, mister – could you? Please.'

The corporeal works of mercy, Farissey thought with irony as he located the levonorgestrel. Back on the street he asked her if she had any money.

'What for, like?'

He flipped her a pound. 'Get yourself a coffee in Val's and have a good think about what you're doing with your life.'

'Take me for a drink, mister?'

A child, as once before, a child. Just play-acting.

'Get yourself along.' He smiled as she skipped out of sight. Going where? Who knows? To a lad who'd just been granted an invisible reprieve? What lad?

He filled out a form accounting for the missing morning-after pill. He had his own reservations about abortion. But when did life start? And when did it end? What's getting killed here? A tiny snake sucking on an egg.

Dolores's recent words came to mind. *Motherhood and murder.* Phrases from his hypnosis session assailed him. *So cold, a scalpel nearly; like drowning, her mother, lost; how sticky, how warm, you wouldn't think; she thinks he must be going for her groin; that's when the pain hits, God above, from the inside out; at that moment she knew she'd never be a mother.*

Why had Dolores set pregnancy against the murder? At first, Farissey though it was a bitchy reference to Victoria's abortion. Motherhood + murder = abortion. But he couldn't see it, not even from that aunt to whom cruelty came as naturally and generously as love. The idea started forming just then.

He sat back in his office chair, asked himself whether Dolores really was the psychic that those crushed souls once paid her to be. *Motherhood and murder.* Farissey let the words work on him like a mantra. He thought himself into a trance, a state of remote viewing.

The killer hadn't had sex with Christina; he only attacked her from the waist up. He wasn't killing her but rather what she might become: everything in her that could mother. Panic had perverted his pure intent. He clearly hadn't wished to see the frenzy to which he succumbed mirrored in eyes of juries, forensics, the dead prostitute herself, and certainly not in the savaged corpse, imprecision carved dismayingly into its flesh and – unlike stone or clay, which can be remoulded, its structure revised or even discarded – resident for all time in diagram, photograph and forensic description. A plot so far botched as to all but obliterate its seal, its signature and maker's mark. No work so fixed; no execution so faltering; no hand so unsteady, ungoverned. Here the art is in the act, the form in its performing, and the killer had failed in every singular duty of a design so fastidious and occult that only the most curious of sensibilities were summoned to its unfolding.

It was largely a matter of pride, that of the artist over the artisan, the nocturnal delicacy of the surgeon over the bucolic, dawn-flushed glee of the butcher. Her breasts should never have been stabbed but cleanly sliced so as to flatten her torso. Her belt was buckled around blue jeans, her two shredded T-shirts stuck to her body, her bra had been driven into her breasts and bone cartilage. That black leather jacket slung beside the mattress and the discarded patent-leather slip-ons were sole testimony to an undressing she herself had freely enacted and he had intervened to forestall.

He didn't want Christina to take her clothes off. He hadn't wanted to use or abuse her gender but to remove it, to take from her all that might in its turn engender, killing the mother in her before the woman, the woman before the whore, the whore before the person, perhaps even the person before the girl, the very girl whose angular and budding essence he may well have sought to restore, redress.

BUTETOWN, 1989: SUMMER

Chapter Ten

The third of July was the day that Loudon Hargest set for the meeting with Farissey and JD. It would turn out to be the hottest of a summer in which the sunlight had fallen in the same overripe, golden and unshadowing fashion, as though night were just an interval in the stream of a steady, unchanging, ever-renewing essence. Clouds were static as though some invisible hand had whipped them into a creamy buoyancy. The grey of the estuary waters became a shock of blue. Everything hung on the unmoving air with a sense of necessity, almost as though the force that propels time onwards had halted, intimating a different order of being, something beyond striving or change.

Public speculations about Christina's death and the Baja brothers ceased as the trial loomed. Butetowners began asking themselves 'What if they are acquitted?'; 'What if word of my disloyalty gets back to the Bajas?'; 'What if we all turn out to be wrong and it's not us who's judging them but them judging us – on a street corner, an alleyway, or just across the street, waiting?' The people of Butetown moved through those cloying days as if through the shimmers of dream or mock tableau. All comings and goings were marked and silently pondered. Everyone was content to watch and wait as word of another summer of love trickled downcountry and 'Ride on Time' blared from cars, consoles, nightclubs and morning radios.

The sky-blue transit pulled up on the Hayes Island at 6.50. JD clambered down, a cigar in his mouth. He had on a black trilby, a blue blazer. He was aloof and affable as they sauntered the Wyndham Arcade, once a place of joke shops, greasy pinball cafés, pawnbrokers, cobblers and humorous tailors, now of iron-shuttered hardware shops and unisex hair salons. The two men stepped tentatively into Kiwi's Bar. It was the coppers' bar in the city centre, its bouncers surplus to requirements and only distinguishable from the regulars by their dicky bows.

'I can't get a piss in the sink for dirty dishes,' Loudon Hargest said in the alcove as they settled to pints of strong lager. 'Fighting a one-on-one war with that fucker Carl Baja for twenty years and look where it's got me.'

Hargest's head left little room in the alcove. Farissey was surprised again by that Adam's apple like a ball-bearing and a neck you'd scarcely get your hands around.

'He thinks it's Pat Garrett and Billy the fucking Kid. Before we arrested him, he found out my home phone number. Kept challenging me to a straight fight – no weapons, no backup. Three o'clock in the morning he was ringing! My old tart was going crazy about it.'

'I'm sure she was, Loudon,' JD said, surveying the bar, looking out for potential setups. Farissey sat back in his chair, closed his eyes, concentrated.

'That Carl Baja was ready to kill me in the police station and I was ready to kill him.' Hargest knew Baja would have gone for him were his hands not tied. Instead, Baja gobbed at Hargest repeatedly. It took three officers to hold Hargest back. 'He's a fucking animal but thank God they restrained me. It'd have messed things up but I'd give anything to have a good crack at him.'

'Way I see it, you've got a lot in common,' JD chided.

'The only thing we've got in common is that we want to do

each other, JD. And I did him – looked that way until those blood tests. And if those bastard brothers walk, it'll finish me and it'll finish everything I've done to clean up Butetown. Get it ready for the redevelopment, for Cardiff Bay, for Europe, for whatever they want to do with the fucking place. And I got him; I nailed him; I put through the arrests. And everybody was well fucking happy. Especially the top brass. All tied up: signed, sealed and fucking delivered.'

'You wouldn't have got them close if it wasn't for me,' JD said. Farissey looked up. JD was biting at the ends of his cigar, a sure sign of how nervous he was.

'Well, you should have given it the works in court. Said you saw them coming out of the flat with blood on their clothes, blood on their hands. Whatever it took. Say you *knew* they did it.'

'That wasn't the deal, Loudon, remember? Deal was, we put you in the right place, put you on to the whole scene. Then all you had to do was make everything fit the picture while we slipped out of it.'

'All right.' Hargest backed off awhile, knowing it was true, and further that JD was his only hope. 'So – you're willing to testify that you saw the Bajas in that room, doing what comes naturally to them? We'll go over it detail by detail, inch by inch of that fucking murder room.'

'No way, Loudon,' JD said. Farissey could hear anger rising in JD's voice. 'I've done what I was supposed to do. I never even liked that. I had to keep reminding myself of the time they batted my nephew. It's not right, besides.'

'You're not fucking moralising with me, now? Are you, JD?' Hargest raised his voice theatrically. He wanted the whole bar to hear.

'Way I see it,' Hargest boomed, 'there's two men here who haven't killed a young girl and one who has.'

Korea. Eyes closed, Farissey tried to see the scene. Paddy fields, a young Korean girl carrying her baby on her head. Looking for some food, she strays into the no-go zone. Shoot once, shoot twice, shoot three times. JD's Enfield .303 bolting from hands that hadn't yet turned twenty years . . . the girl going down, the baby up into the air.

Opening his eyes, Farissey saw JD leaned back in his seat, arms folded across his chest. The blood had drained from his face. 'Orders were orders in those days, you know that, Loudon. Shoot once, shoot twice. Third time you knew they meant it.'

'I don't mean to get heavy,' Hargest said, softly now, running his arm round the back of JD's seat. 'I respect what you did in Korea – who wouldn't? Fuck, JD, you don't need me to tell you that. You got medals to show what you did for us.' Hargest paused, lowered his arm on to JD's shoulder. 'But Korea was nearly a lifetime ago. You got to be good for more than nostalgia.'

JD looked overwhelmed in this alcove, by this talk. He sipped on his pint, drew on his cigar, collected himself. 'I was just a boy in Korea . . . So, say what you like, Loudon, say. There isn't a thing else I'm prepared to do.'

'Well, fuck you, too, JD. I'll have your bollocks for earrings, you wait.' Hargest pulled JD's cigar out of his mouth. He held it towards JD as though he was going to stub it into his eyes. 'Forty-odd years we've known each other.' He dropped the cigar into JD's pint.

Hargest turned on Farissey. 'How about you?'

'Same as JD.'

'Damn you, damn you both,' he said, leaving. 'I'll go about this my own fucking way.'

'You go alone, Loudon. That's right for you,' JD said.

Farissey and JD sat in silence, all eyes along the long bar fixed on them.

'Many a tear has to fall,' JD crooned, back in the blue transit. He turned over the engine. It was the balmiest of evenings, the sky a pendulous mauve. To the west, the sun trailed pools of indigo. Farissey wondered if he'd ever seen such a sunset over Cardiff.

'Let's just drive around for a bit,' JD suggested.

So, the van crawls along Bute Street. Outside the steel-shuttered Loudoun Square shopping centre, a few teenage black kids are sitting knees to chin. A tall white woman passes by. The adolescents look at her – Farissey can't know how – disdainful, lustful, envious. Further down, four cute little black boys are hoisting a fifth over the railway line's wall.

As they drove, JD talked about those days before he and Loudon Hargest went to Korea. Things had a sense of reality then. The cops and criminals had respect for each other: their antagonism was fierce, but sporting and sparkling with humour. He talked about a Chinese restaurateur who dealt opium. The police couldn't figure how he got it off the boats. After years of investigation, they discovered he used messenger pigeons. Hargest had just started as a bobby. The Chinaman moonlighted when Hargest tipped him off.

'Birmingham, the Chinaman went. Good luck to him and his sly smile,' JD said, lighting a cigar.

He drove on aimlessly but with unconscious care. He commented on the cityscape, anticipated the next moves of the Dockland's Regeneration Corporation in its design to make the docks into 'the Venice of the North'. A builder's lore told him what they were doing, what the brief was at the highest level of design. Widen all the roads to give the impression of space, of desolate and windswept beauty. 'What a load of fucking bollocks,' JD exclaimed. He laughed aloud at the wheel of his transit van, a van not big enough to make his laugh, his bulk and presence seem unconstrained.

JD swerved off Bute Street into Loudoun Square and parked behind the estate pub, the Bosun. Farissey opened his shirt, pulled off the masking tape, winced and smiled as it ripped hairs out of his chest. The cassette would have caught all JD's whistling and singing and laughing and talking in the van.

'Well, that might be a bit of fun too,' JD said as he pulled out the cassette, took a biro from his shirt pocket and wrote: 'James Vincent Dwyer/John "Jack" Malachi Farissey/Loudon Hargest: Kiwi's, 7:20 p.m., 3/7/89.' For more devilment, JD put the cassette back into the machine and sang an off-key rendition of Marvin Gaye's 'I Need a Witness' at the slow-spinning, congested wheels.

Farissey put the tape into a padded envelope, wrote 'URGENTLY, Madieson and Madieson Solicitors' on its cover. 'You ready for this, JD? Hargest will be on our backs – we know that. But Carl isn't going to see us as saviours either.'

JD scarcely seemed to be listening. A smile passed across his broad face, an older smile, one of resignation. The Big Man wasn't thinking about the Bajas or Loudon Hargest. He was thinking of fried chicken, of endless pints of Brains Dark, of Dolores and another day's dawning.

In the heat of the following afternoon, Lida was sitting in Farissey's front room.

'I've done that deal with the police to get me out of here,' Lida said. 'I'll be off in a month or so: they haven't said where yet. It's a fucking weight off my mind. Thanks. You're the only one who's done something that counts.'

'It's nothing,' Farissey said. 'Thank JD if you want to thank anyone. Does Josie know?'

'No. Only you and him and the coppers.'

'Keep it that way,' he said, tossing her another can of Red Stripe. She caught it with girlish surprise.

'How's your missus doing?' Her tones were sardonic.

'Twenty weeks,' he said. 'She's in perfect health.'

'She's over the worst of it, then. It'll happen now. How about you?'

He smiled, shrugged, noticed that she'd put a lot of heavy eye make-up on. How pale she looked, how terrified through those always open and tiredly beautiful eyes, eyes that had looked too long and too hard for their nineteen years. He'd make her easy for today anyway, give her those eight hours of ecstatic near-sleep towards which all organisms aspire as to a memory, a garden, a time of grace.

He watched two gulls gymnasting in the mist and wondered whether he didn't love Lida, not sexually but as he might love a daughter or cherished pet. How changed she was from when he first met her, him slumped across the counter of the North Star and her saying: 'This dickhead says he's a poet of the sea. Get a fucking load of this, Tina.' He'd liked her more than Christina straight off. Lida was cajoling and tender where Christina struck him as calculating, dispassionate, flighty and affronted by his gaze.

'After we've drunk these we'll go see the French guys down the road,' Farissey said, breaking a silence. 'Up the stakes a bit, just for a day.'

'What the fuck do we do if the Bajas are released?' she'd asked. She'd become quite dependent on him now that she'd been ostracised from the scene.

'We'll do something nice,' he'd said. 'Whether they get out or not.' He'd organised a £50 heroin deal for himself and Lida.

Two French Algerians were staying in a rented house on the Clarence Embankment. They were students, though Farissey never saw them doing much apart from drugs as they sensibly shifted around between smack and coke and speed and downs, so as to skirt specific addictions. 'Butterflies never get pinned,' Eric said. He intrigued Farissey; a death-haunted young hippie, silent, astute when he did speak, and gracious in gesture. He was twenty-four, his liver already devastated from three bouts of hepatitis. One time, he'd gone drinking with Farissey and the session cost him five days in bed with liver crisis. Farissey took him back to the flat a few times to slip him some clean works. Victoria disapproved of Eric. 'Life's wasted on people like that,' she'd said.

Eric and Alain picked up their heroin from somewhere in King's Cross. Farissey had tried their gear once and found it a thousand times better than anything you could score in Cardiff. He'd asked them to get enough smack for two people to take it right to the point just before death, along that curious asymptotic path that has claimed as many justified corpses as transported souls.

*

'I smoked it but I never shot smack before,' Lida said in the street. 'Still, I'm going to all sorts of places I never been at the moment,' she murmured, taking Farissey's arm on the short walk down the Clarence Embankment.

'Don't worry about the smack and don't worry about the Bajas,' Farissey said.

The River Taff was alive for once, talking in muddy gurgles. A curlew wheeled and dived in the welcome wind.

'Jack, uhm?' She didn't use his name often. Her avoidance of proper names was one of the things in her that Farissey found so congenial, so respectful. 'You could see me wherever it is I'm going, couldn't you? . . . I'd like that.'

'You've got my phone number. Be sure to get *me*, though. Three rings and wait ten minutes before calling back.'

The students' window was wide open in the heatwave. Farissey and Lida jockeyed into the room, where Eric was sitting cross-legged in front of a face mirror. A Jif lemon, a little run of string and a bag of heroin squatted between his legs. Eric introduced them to his friend Alain. 'His English, it is not very good,' he said. 'He is – how you say? – pregnant with silence.'

There was nothing on the walls and no furniture, apart from a mattress, a record player, two dozen albums, a naked lightbulb and some curtains, in this front room made into a bedroom. A limp, half-full and seemingly mobile rubbish bag sat slug-like in the room's corner.

'You are wanting to do it all now?' Eric asked. He was already heavily smacked up, staggering a little but more like a corner-bound boxer than a drunk.

'Yeah. A bit more for me and a bit less for Lida – you know.' Farissey went to take the needle.

'Different, here. Much different,' Eric said.

'Only part of my training.' Farissey shrugged amiably. He tourniqueted his arm, pumped it like an athlete training with a dumbbell.

Eric liquidised a four-inch line of smack with the Jif and drew it into the needle. As he injected Farissey, Eric pulled away to be sick in the rubbish bag.

'Don't worry,' Alain said to Lida. 'Is normal. Perfectly natural.'

Farissey looked at the needle in his arm: an unnatural tree with rich, bloody boughs.

'Good veins,' Eric said to Farissey, having resumed his station and now drawing blood into the needle.

Farissey watched his blood go out and his blood come back in. Seconds later it hit his head. He doesn't know what he's said but he feels like a leaf falling endlessly into a chasm of pleasures, the only refuge from a world where willing has no Sabbath, where the wheel and its fire never once still or cease.

Lida joins him on the mattress some indefinable time later. He holds her until they must both vomit ecstatically into the rubbish bag that was itself a sack of vomit. The beer and a little food rose orgasmically like hairs abristle a stroked arm, gentle as lover's shadows flung elegant by streetlamplight on the pavement. And then prone, open-eyed, dreaming, he lay with this labile girl, flaxen, limpid, gamine-dark, pale and blood and bruise-mottled, and himself wondering where there were no words, no knowing, and the imponderable could be held with clarity and tenderness.

'Don't roll a spliff,' Lida lisped, as he moved towards his papers and hash. 'Leave your hand on my head.' She sighed, closed her eyes, hummed some tune quietly to herself. 'Don't you like me that way?'

'I do. It's just not right. Besides, like you say, I've got to get domesticated now.'

Eric and Alain rolled up Farissey's gift of hash, gazing down like kind matchmakers on tonight's couple.

'Never so good for us as them – it's a beginning drug,' Eric says to Alain.

Eric threw a shirt over the lightbulb and the whole room reflected the softening sublime, the lucid flight of distinction and category it had been the drug's genie to launch. Somebody could die in here without a finger being lifted. Too much hassle to call out people in uniforms, death being more kindly, more clement than officialdom, those savages arriving with a sense of

self sanctioned by an office, a station, a mission. For that afternoon and evening, Farissey again felt everything he had longed
to feel and which it had been his greater misfortune to recall:
eight hours of nirvana in the world's room.

At one in the morning they thank Eric and Alain wordlessly
and pick up a taxi to King's Snooker on the garishly vibrant St
Mary's Street. Off limits now. Trawling, brooding, in the neon
alcoves of the town centre. 'I'll do a little business up here,' Lida
says. She only manages two hand jobs in the lavatories and for
the rest of the night they drink slowly, drain off the smack fix
and silently make plans for a world malcontent and laconically
in wait.

BUTETOWN, 1989: AUTUMN

'It is the dead,
Not the living, who make the longest demands.
We die for ever . . .'
Sophocles, *Antigone*

Chapter Eleven

Farissey watched and waited as the prosecution case against the Bajas crumbled. There was a daily carnival around the law court: a shuffling, shouting chaos of civil rights activists, Nation of Islam representatives, class warriors, the soldiers of Inited Idren and tracksuited soul sisters making show of their loyalty to the Baja brothers.

He watched the scenes following the acquittal on the early-evening news. Carl Baja's voice was unsteady as he spoke to the cameras. 'I wasn't there when my boy says his first sentences. There's some people in Butetown should suffer like I did. Then maybe they'd learn to tell the truth.' Baja's face seemed to take up the entire screen: stern yet explosive, the skin over that broad face looking like a paper bag just holding back a torrent of blood.

It was a close day in early September when a subdued Carl Baja insisted on talking in the back room of the pharmacy. Prison had been easy enough for Baja, Farissey learned. It had been comfortable even. But when Baja had reunited with his wife, his mother, his children and his alsatian, and had experienced the surreal savour of again walking through women-filled streets, he began a struggle with an enemy he'd never expected to make.

Baja had first encountered his demon on a shopping expedition with his wife, Pauline. Turning the corner into St Mary's Street, he froze before the flocks of people, the length of road stretching as far as his eyes could see. The skies, so very, very high, dwarfed and overcame him. He'd come out of prison into the great immensity of things, into a world he'd always taken for granted. He feigned dizziness and asked his wife if they might return to their cramped Butetown home, to the clutter of prams, playpens, videos and toys. His choice of alibi was not arbitrary, Farissey suspected. The terrible vertigo of being had overcome him.

The phrase 'get on with my life' came to Carl Baja's mind often. The word 'life' jumped out, reverberated in his ears, shocked him with a new challenge, a mystery or threat. He looked at the sky with dread. What was the sky? he asked. The question convulsed through him like a minor seizure. He felt as if he was abruptly awakening to every new fact, event, situation.

Baja had looked at the houses and buildings of Butetown, realised that none of it was home. Once, this had all been field or mud or sea. He knew that he walked through an illusion. A horror of the primeval, of the baseless ground, was all of him, all of his days. Had he education, he might have turned to philosophy or mysticism. Instead, he resumed his cocaine habit, used moderately and for hauteur, not highs; confidence, not kickstarts. His determination that no one should detect this core of weakness within meant that he made the most of any venture into the dreadful outdoors. It also meant that he was set on showing Butetown, Loudon Hargest, and the mocking voices he suspected on every airwave, that he had come out harder, cleverer and more feudal than ever. And for the moment that involved doing precisely nothing.

On the tenth day following his acquittal, Carl Baja grew to trust the night. He reincarnated his night self for public view on Caroline Street. He stood alone but for the leadless alsatian roaming his background. He was black-suited, his neck enor-

mous in a lilac polo-neck sweater. He gazed down on the narrow
2.15 a.m. zoo of chippies, kebab houses, shuttered porn shops
and seedy pseudo-restaurants as if at a lake of dirty grease and
hungers.

What was he looking for? Perhaps he was just looking for the
sake of looking, as he couldn't when prone hour upon hour on a
harsh bed amid those high walls that turned his gaze inwards,
perhaps on an angry absence. His gaze was awesome and
majestic, but strangely weary, laden, as athletes and warriors are
said to be before the effort. A look like Sonny Liston, leering at
a kingdom below as it spun out of his control.

Two Armenian taxi drivers stood at the door of Dorothy's
Fish Bar.

'What's he doing up in town?' the younger Armenian was
whispering to the elder. 'Why doesn't he stay down the docks?
He can do what he wants down there.'

'Why didn't he go down for that prostitute? That's what I
want to know,' lisped the older of the two.

'What's he going to do next is more to the point,' the younger
Armenian countered.

'No telling with people like him,' rejoined the elder.

The older Armenian was right, in ways he couldn't have
foreseen. Each dawn for four days, three bunches of cheap
flowers appeared outside the Angelina Street flat. Word got
about. The bored, the sleepless, those minded for the macabre
made vigils in the small hours. No one saw anyone putting the
flowers down. Perhaps they're coming from inside the building,
people speculated. Everyone took it ominously. In the way of the
docks. The way of the powerless.

Two weeks later, the defence team put on a party to celebrate
the Bajas' acquittal and to thank everyone who had contributed
to the effort. The venue was the Bute Dock, a lemon and red bar
in West Bute Street, newly refurbished in a sad attempt at an
office workers' rendezvous in an area where clerical staff dashed
for the earliest city-centre-bound train.

Farissey spent the hour beforehand at Lida's house. Lida

seemed tranquil as she prospected the bleak adventure that was to unfold in the hours after Josie left the house to face the Bajas.

He gave Josie Marshall sleeping pills, as arranged. She thanked him distractedly, paced around the flat, finding fault with Lida over the state of the kitchen, the baby's clothes, the unmade bed, the stinking fucking sheets. 'Who's got the fear worse, me or her?' Lida whispered while Josie was in the kitchen.

'If you've got something to say, say it,' insisted Lida when Josie paced back into the front room. Lida was sprawled on the couch: taunting, vampish.

'Say, say? What do I fucking say to Carl Baja? "Me I knew she was lying, but I still keeps on living with the bitch." How's that going to sound – full of shit or what?'

'Say anything you can, love. Blame me. Say you fucking hates me, but you stays around to look after the baby. Say you thought the baby might die if it was left with me. Carl Baja might believe that: everyone knows you loves the baby.'

'I could,' Josie said, lighting a cigarette and getting down on to her haunches. 'But I wouldn't have to be saying nothing if you hadn't shat yourself with the police.'

'I knew they was going to get the Bajas one way or another. So I'm thinking what's the point of me going down too and everyone thinking that I helps kill my best friend, who I loves, I fucking loves?' She shouldn't have said that, Farissey thought. Anything about Christina drove Josie spare. Absolutely fucking spare.

'Fucking lies, lies, lies. That's all anyone gets from you. Fucking lies.'

'I was scared, Josie. I was fucking petrified. All I wants is to get back here, get back to you and the baby.'

'We all gets fucking scared,' Josie growls. 'What you does when you gets scared, that's what you are. And you showed what you are, Lida.'

'I didn't think it'd make no difference. The coppers was going to fuck the boys up anyway,' Lida says, still languorous, blowing out cigarette smoke with vague contempt.

'And what do they use to fuck them up? Your fucking lies. Like they passes you this knife and you stick it in her ribs.'

'Fucking stop it, Josie. Fucking stop it, all right. The coppers says all that to me. They feeds it all to me. I just says "yes sir, yes sir, yes sir – three bags full." '

'It's "no sir, no sir, no sir, three bags full of nothing said", you stupid fucking cow.'

A quarter of an hour later, Josie was ready to leave for the acquittal party. She'd tried to make herself look smart. A green trouser suit: squat, ill-fitting, out of fashion; poor Josie.

'Sorry, Josie, really. I means it,' Lida said at the door, the baby slung over her shoulder.

'Bit late now.' Josie kissed the baby on the back of his head, squeezed his cheeks. 'See you later, little man.'

'No you won't,' Lida whispered as Josie strode off determinedly in her trouser suit, an indistinct green shape as she turned right on to Angelina Street.

Warm, generous tears ran down Lida's cheeks. She and Farissey moved quickly. Within twenty minutes, three holdalls were next to the door. Lida left some things behind, stole a few of Josie's, as it seemed useful, appropriate. She snorted a heavy line of sulphate off the kitchen table. The speed stopped her from being tearful, jumbled up her sadnesses.

What the fuck was Bristol to her? she asked. A splurge of fucking roads and houses. And how the fuck was she going to start hustling again? They don't run fucking nurseries for her lot. Got to find a bloke or a girl straight off: go for some ugly fucker who's glad of it and'll stop in nights. Make up some fucking bullshit about a bar job until she's well set up with a bunch of twenties. Find someone better then. Build it all up from scratch. Start over. She could do it. She could go on. Fuck the lot of them. Fuck her mam. Fuck her the most. She'd read that fucking interview thing in the local paper where her mam disowned her. Stupid, selfish bitch had done that when she gave birth. At least Lida kept her baby close to her. Right at her chest; the only thing left in the world. She looked at little Daryl, chewing at her jumper. Poor, stupid, sweet little thing. Don't know we're going away, don't know nothing. We'll do it. We can do it. We'll go on.

She fell silent, sat chain-smoking at the kitchen window, the baby now asleep in his pushchair on the black and grey tiled floor. She smoked each cigarette halfway down, folded one out and reached into a pack of Embassy Regal for another. The ashtray overflowing, spilled ash, two empty cans of Breaker: these things would be the last Josie would see of her.

The kitchen curtains lit up with car headlights at eight in the evening. Seven-thirty, the police had said. To coincide with the Bute Dock party. 'All your enemies will be in there,' Hargest had told Lida over the phone. He'd sounded angry with her and with everyone. 'So no one will notice you slipping off with us.' She was an embarrassment to them now, a reminder of just how badly they'd fucked up. They'd agreed to drive her to Bristol, pay for two weeks in a bed and breakfast. After that she was on her own.

Loudon Hargest was in the passenger seat. Neither he nor the driving policeman got out of the car.

'Don't look back,' Farissey whispered to Lida at the car door. 'You've got to hold it together.' *This must have been where Christina lost her nerve, going to England for the first time.*

'Sick of carrying corpses,' says Hargest as Lida settles herself on the back seat, rocks the baby to abate its low grizzling. The two policemen grumble about having to go to bastard Bristol then about the party at the Bute Dock. What's anybody doing celebrating those two getting off? Victims of the system! Every-one'd soon see who the victims were and who the villains were.

Lida doesn't look back at the house as the car starts up. When the car will turn out of Butetown, she won't look back. That's all over now; like Tina, like her and Josie, like the Custom House and the North Star. New pitches, new punters, new accents in front of her.

Something gone from my world, too, Farissey thought as he made his way to the Bute Dock.

*

The party was dismal. Lines had been drawn even in the first hour: journalists, liberals and SWP members on one side; local supporters, Baja associates and family on the other. The latter group cast the odd glances of tolerant contempt across the room, as if to say 'you helped get the brothers off, and for that we've got to accept you, but don't even think to tell us what's what down here or what any of this means'. It was almost a black and white line. Farissey noticed Josie Marshall tiptoeing the line, hoping to get a word in with Carl Baja.

Everyone remarked on how quickly Baja had lost the weight he'd put on in prison. Baja put it down to a change in diet, all the time concealing the fact that in prison he had recaptured that sense of childhood safety that left his life with his father's death.

He came across to Victoria, kissed her hand solemnly. 'Someone should have organised a blues for tonight,' he said. 'I used to run a few myself, you know. It's something to look forward to round here.'

'Yeah – it's all a bit flat and sort of wrong, this,' she said.

'Look at my brother over there, skinning up with hustlers,' Carl said, staring at the small group surrounding Tony Baja in the corner of the bar. 'I likes a smoke and that myself, but there's a proper time and place. Anyway,' Carl continued, 'I remembers how you comes to see us in prison. It cheered me up, seeing a woman.'

'Well, that wasn't why I was there,' she replied sharply.

Baja paused, looking down on her, as if reading her thoughts. 'There's more to seeing women than ideas of fucking,' his expression said. 'Especially inside: another place you never been.' There was a strange quality in his eyes, a barely doused fire.

'Nice dress,' Carl Baja says of Victoria's knee-length red and black crepe. She didn't believe in those flowing, disguising things. Made it all somehow taboo like those tribes who kept menstruating women out of the kitchen.

'I think I'll get my wife one like that. You should meet her.'

'We met, during the trial,' Victoria says, looking at Pauline

Baja, a young light-skinned woman who is not just pretty, but precise and dignified, a child at each hand.

'You're pregnant. Nice to see, my love. Can't be long now.'

'Yeah. It's due in about two months.'

'I wants to see my wife pregnant again. You looks strong.' He looked at her with some strange rectitude. 'When you have that kid, I'd like to see it. Maybe once a year. Watch it grow up.'

Carl Baja stood a round, asked Farissey to accompany him to the bar. At the bar, Baja invoked their shared schooldays. 'All that time. Where does it all go?'

As Farissey pondered the question, he noticed Tony Baja sidling across to Victoria. Tony placed his hand on her shoulder, offered her a hit on a joint. She shook her head, looked away. Tony's hand moved down her back. She pushed his hand away. Across the other side of the room, Farissey could see Tony's new girlfriend looking 'bitch' right through Victoria.

Pauline Baja got to Tony first. She whispered something in Tony's ear. He backed off, cupping the joint behind him like a reluctant mourner outside a church.

'Sorry about that,' Pauline said to Farissey and Victoria. 'Carl says we've got to sort him about these things. Bit late in the day if you ask me . . . Anyway, thanks for all that work you did for us. Especially when—' she smiles, looking at Victoria's belly – 'you know.'

She was the same height as Victoria. They were both slim, fine-gestured and olive-skinned. They talked about the trial, then about pregnancy. As they talked, Farissey saw Victoria's smile return to her. He noticed how Pauline's clothes had a well-tended, oft-worn quality. She made the best of a cheap black top, brought it to life with a silver necklace and a tasteful cardigan. There was an exotic air of absolute fidelity about this woman. Farissey could envisage Pauline Baja in wartime, become a market trader or nocturnal seamstress.

Carl returned with an orange juice and soda for Victoria. She asked if there'd been some mix-up with the order.

'I changes it,' he smiled. 'I suppose you got confused in all the excitement. Pauline didn't even have wine in the cooking when she was pregnant. I even went outside to smoke a fag. Someone's got to look out for them.'

'Tony's up to his old tricks,' Pauline said. 'He was coming on to Victoria.'

'You shouldn't have to put up with that,' Carl said to Victoria. 'I'll have a word with him.'

Victoria began gathering up glasses and ashtrays, consciously winding the party down even as the music droned on. Pauline Baja lent a hand, observing Victoria all the while.

An argument broke out. Carl Baja grabbed his brother by the lapels, pushed him up against the amplifiers on the stage. Released, Tony pirouetted off to take his girfriend's arm. As they left, the girlfriend broke from his arm and minced up to Victoria.

'That's fucking it?' she shouted: a girl, not yet a woman, wearing a silver shirt, a red tutu dress, high stilettos, something Sicilian or Algerian in her features. The girl looked Victoria up and down.

'You, you . . .' she shouts. 'Don't fucking ignore me. And don't think Tone fancies you one fucking bit, darling. It was just a setup, all right. So Carl could do his big knight in shining armour bit.'

'I didn't think anything of it,' Victoria retorted.

'Tone not fucking good enough for you, no? Well, that's your problem. Just so you knows, I ain't worried.'

But she *is* worried, the little girl. Farissey could tell from those eyes full of jealousy, self-doubt, maybe other worries too. Everyone's play-acting. Something painful, even lethal in here tonight, Farissey thinks as Victoria exchanges phone numbers with Pauline Baja.

'That little slut won't bother you,' said Pauline quietly. 'We're at 16 Louisa Place if you needs anything. Anything at all.'

Fifteen minutes later, Farissey left Victoria with the defence team. He went back to his flat. The phone rang three times. Ten minutes later, he was listening to a drunk, half-speeding Lida.

Hargest had put her into a place called the Hotel Avon, right in the heart of St Paul's, Bristol's red-light district.

'Fair enough,' she said. 'I'm not going to find work anywhere else. Do all right at first, too. New kid on the block and all that.'

'How about money for now?'

'Fine. I got a little windfall.'

She explained that the owner of the hotel was a bloke of about fifty with glasses and a red face. Seemed a bit shaky, had that pervy, faraway stare. Hargest asked him if he's still reading books. Learning books. ABC and all that. Boy Scout manuals. Still passing them around in his circle. The owner went into a back room; he came back with a stuffed white envelope.

Outside, Hargest told Lida to stand out of sight of the hotel and the police car. What the fuck's this? she thought, shaking now. She felt tears, more human than anything the speed shakes out of you. Lida couldn't figure how Hargest was looking at her. He reached into his pocket, opened the white envelope and counted off £280 from a roll.

'You're in for two weeks,' Hargest said. 'If that cunt charges you any, let me know.'

'Thanks,' Lida responded, 'thanks.' Something had rooted her to the spot. All warmth coming up from her chest, her head swimming; like a lovely, uncut fix.

Farissey put down the phone. He drank a glass of wine, reflected on Lida's last words before she ran out of coins for the payphone. 'All hustling,' she'd said. 'Good hustling, bad hustling.'

The next day, Farissey awoke to hear an alien chatter at the foot of the stairs. He was struck by the easy atmosphere between Victoria and Pauline Baja as the latter brought in a mass of hand-me-downs. He helped bring in cots, highchairs, a shopping bag of unopened nappies, six baby gros in pinks and reds and tartan.

'Got the day off?' Pauline asked searchingly. 'Don't look so well, Jack.'

'Just the tail end of a bit of flu,' he lied. 'I'm in the shop this afternoon.'

'Should take better care of yourself,' she said. 'Need all your strength when the baby comes along.'

He made coffees, found some lemonade for the children. He offered Pauline a cigarette. He lit his own, retreated to the bedroom and left Pauline and Victoria to talk what might have been birdsong but for a flat, meaningless profundity in their tones, like rural girls sharing impenetrable wisdoms over a smallholding.

'It's just what we need, Jack,' Victoria said after thanking Pauline Baja at the door. Victoria ruffled up his hair as she might an adored child. 'She's so nice.'

'She is,' Farissey agreed. 'But she won't divide loyalties.'

'You don't think it's like a judgement on you? Like you're not thinking about these things.'

'No, just a judgement on the world at large,' he said, some inexplicable languor settling on him as he descended the stairs.

It was an easy afternoon's work, most customers coming in for over-the-counter medications: hangover cures, vitamin tablets or items of hygiene. He found time to write letters to doctors where he suspected misdiagnosis.

He also found time to add a few paragraphs to his paper for the *Pharmacopoeia*. Silymarin, he wrote, was the active agent in milk thistle which protected the liver against toxic damage. 'While the foregoing does not address the ultimate causes of liver dysfuction – i.e. addiction, genetic susceptibility – it may well bolster the work of the gamma enzyme.'

He enjoyed this part of his work, sparse though it was. Most of the time his occupation was no more than a base declension of arithmetic. Counting for orders, counting for preparations. The pharmacist had once practised an art and a science and a craft. He was entrusted with the extemporaneous preparation of medicines, of bougies, pills, plasters and potions. Nowadays his art, like that of cobblers, shoemakers and jewel–cutters, had been eaten away by multinationals. It was left to Farissey only to advise and explain, to ensure that dosage forms were correct and to stand guarantor for the quality and efficacy of the prescription.

At four o'clock, his assistant passed through a prescription: '250 × 10mg diazepam. 500 × 30mg temazapam. Mr Carl Baja.' Farissey saw the whole scam in a flash. Baja had added zeros. He estimated that Baja could get a prescription only every two months. That gives me time to weigh things up, Farissey thought.

Carl Baja was motionless at the counter in a black leather jacket and white shirt. He made the shop look cramped. Farissey's assistant pretended to be busy rearranging the vitamin display, her nerves on edge.

'This once, Carl,' Farissey whispered at the door. 'Just this once.'

At six o'clock, Farissey walked to Angelina Street to witness a press conference the Bajas had organised outside the murder flat. Ten minutes later, the Bajas pulled up outside the Angelina Street flat in two small cars. Tony and his acerbic little girlfriend got out first. Pauline was driving the other car. Carl was in the back, two children clambering over him like aggrieved little animals.

All bore impressive wreaths, the children included. The wreaths were made to match their bearers, like they'd been cut and arranged according to shoe sizes.

'Say our thing, Tone,' Carl said, backing away from the cameras.

'We are today laying flowers outside the flat in which Christina Villers was murdered,' Tony read from a handwritten note. 'This is a gesture of respect to her memory and to her family. It is also a reminder that the real killer has not yet been found and that the police investigation should be reopened.'

'Do you intend to take legal action against the South Wales police force?' a sandy-haired television reporter asked Tony.

'We've got nothing else to say,' Carl interjected. 'Please allow us to pay our respects.' It sounded like he was quoting lines, too, but the effect was decisive.

Victoria met up with Farissey directly across the road. Quiet gossip and intrigue seemed almost palpable on that sweaty, dreary afternoon. There was a strangely redemptive light in Victoria's eyes as she looked at the wreaths outside the Angelina Street flat and then up to the first-floor room. Sourceless lines were circling around in Farissey's head: *For murder, though it have no tongue, will speak / With most miraculous organ.*

'Well, it was a touching gesture of respect,' Victoria said.

Feeling as though the sky was going to cave in on him, Farissey nodded. 'Perhaps we misjudged the boys all along,' he smiled wearily. 'I wouldn't have thought they were capable of it.'

Respect. Respect the dead. But most of all respect the living – the breathing, the walking, the watching, the looming.

Twenty minutes later, Farissey was alone in the flat. He went through the pile of hand-me-downs from Pauline Baja. What he saw confirmed his suspicions. The cots and chairs were all in perfect condition. The clothes looked shop-clean. The labels on the baby gros read MATALAN – an out-of-town discount megastore which had opened only three months earlier.

Chapter Twelve

For a week, Farissey stayed off the night-trails. He prepared evening meals of aïoli, of devilled kidneys, lamb tagine, grilled whitebait in pepper sauce. He read newspapers, sipped beer or red wine as he waited for Victoria with neither impatience nor repose. He often took to the fire exit, sat in sunsets made scarlet by twenty-six rainless days.

After work on the last Friday of September, he assembled the ingredients for pipérade on the kitchen table. He ran his hand along the bumped wall, polished the range in which he cooked the finely textured casseroles that had formerly been the staple of his sparse diet.

The day was losing its light. He felt darkness insinuate itself round the edges of the bay, the natural loneliness curl around him. His hand reached instinctively for the light switch. He chopped onions, garlic, peppers, parsley, chives and tarragon. He placed the vegetables and herbs into bowls, admired the colours. He was a passable cook, he knew, simply because he was more concerned with the cooking than eating of a dish. He opened a bottle of red wine, took it to the fire exit.

The sun was receding over the neighbouring areas of Grangetown and Riverside. Its light scattered and waned over the houses not like a lament but a tired forgetting, an exhaustion not of its own but of the land itself. Twilight was not the time of shadows, he knew, but the hour when darkness sucks all shadows into itself.

He was halfway through the bottle when she returned. She wore a white jacket and purple beret at odds with her disconnected, edgy mood. Something very simple was what she wanted. He put the vegetable bowls in the fridge, toasted bread. He poached four eggs by creating a vortex in boiling water, watched the eggs slither into the pan, form tails and chase each other in the swirling water.

He heard a bang on the front door, then something tinnily melodious and substantial drop through the letterbox. He turned off the flame, went through the front room. Victoria's beret was tossed across the floor along with the red baby's cardigan she was knitting. He watched as she slipped carefully down the narrow staircase, one hand on the rail. A new tiredness was on her; a gravid feeling, a mental lethargy. She was approaching the eighth month of her pregnancy; the baby was weighing on her.

She returned with a scruffy, smudged white envelope. Both recognised the small, distinctively looped script which announced 'F.A.O. Mrs Victoria Farissey, By Hand'. It contained three keys and a note: a Chubb and a Yale to get into the doors of Jess's flat and a small one which looked like it might open a guitar case. The note read:

Congratulations! You knew I'd fallen out with the Bajas and that I couldn't stay around with them back in Butetown. You and your lawyer friends have forced me out of *my* home town! That hurts as much as anything.

So it's all happy and nearly nuclear families for you and Jack here on in. But you won't forget me. When the time comes, you'll have a daily living breathing shitting crying shaming reminder of *me*. Ask Jack if you don't believe!

I leave you keys because you won't take smiles or rings.

Stay put and stay cool. You haven't heard the last of your Jess.

The last of the sunlight played softly on the water as they entered the Atlantic Wharf development. Jess had stripped the place of everything but tinker's treasure. The dark-oak writing bureau was the only thing left. That's probably where he wrote that note, Farissey thought. The last thing he did before spinning off like a harlequin. The little key unlocked the bureau.

At first what they saw didn't register. It looked like a bunch of slugs, anaemic, translucent slugs, in some strange formation. Bellies of small, glutted animals. Victoria shrieked before knowing why she was shrieking. They all wobbled slightly as Farissey pulled open the drawer. They were living, writhing, liquid and skin. Ugly massed little beasts. Like the shit bags you gut from mackerels.

'You disgusting fucking wanker. You gross insect,' she whispered.

'That's Jess,' Farissey said. 'Always organised in the domestic space.'

They'd all been clipped with white tags: labelled specimens. Precisely stapled to stop the air getting in. Like re-corked wine. One by one, night after night, he'd been recording the names, the pick-up points and dates in a tiny, meticulous hand.

Becky: Wine Bar, Oxford Road 19/12/88
Jackie?: Flanagans, Liverpool 22/12/88
Sue: Hag Bar, West Didsbury 27/12/88
Isobel: Her House, Cardiff 4/1/89
Marjorie: Stairway Cleaner, Atlantic Wharf 21/1/89
Lovely Linda: Kiwi's, Cardiff 22/1/89

She looked sideways, up, down, across: a taxonomy of maggots. More sperm in some than others: something near three hundred of them. Some ochred with menstrual residue. All neatly lined up in chronological order spanning 1980 to 1989. 'There's got to be a limit to the number of twangy vaginas a man wants to experience in a lifetime,' said a smiling Farissey.

Victoria's look killed his smile. 'Could Christina be in among these?' she asked.

Victoria worked through in order, counting, counting until she noticed her own name. Two dozen times or more. 'What the fuck's this?' she asked. 'What the fuck?' Now and then he'd used a condom. Other times, he played that stupid reverse game with the rubbers. But nothing like twenty times: that was the source of this whole hell of a business. But that was the difference, she realised. Just a few of the condoms weren't used, including a few bearing her name. He'd recorded unprotected encounters with opened but unused condoms. The dates made sense. She calculated from a sample.

Victoria: Atlantic Wharf 5/2/89
Victoria: Atlantic Wharf 5/2/89
Victoria: Jack's Flat 10/2/89
Victoria: Sofa – my mother's house 13/2/89

There were no dateless nights – fucks with a date and a signature and a perfume. Fucking slimeball, wanking bastard, she muttered. Fucking wanking prick. That moment of connection between them, he'd said. Slithering fucking semen slugs. If this is your will, your testimony, Jess Simmonds, then it's the perfect account of your slimy soul. She saw the last entry under her name. He'd used a condom then.

'He could have just been wanking in some of these things and added labels.'

'I think it's for real,' replied Farissey. Jess's sneering words: *Always organised in the domestic space. Not like you, Blackjack.*

'What sort of a fucking hobby is that? Why doesn't he collect stamps or something?'

'It's the madeleine,' said Farissey, looking around for a place to flick his ash. He ground it into the carpet. He answered the question in her eyes. 'The madeleine's not a woman. It's a little French cake in Proust's novel.'

'That *Remembrance* thing? I haven't read it.'

'Nor had Jess. See, he had this thing about recalling intensely pleasurable experiences at will. When I was starting out as a pharmacist, I even got hold of some sodium pentothal for him. I told him he should read Proust. He doesn't, of course, but when he tells me what he's doing with his condoms, I think it's pretty amusing – but that was ten years ago.'

'I'm glad someone's amused by this,' she said sharply.

'Well, it's better than getting upset by the number of times you and he . . . and in my flat, for fuck's sake.'

She folded her arms, her poise bolt upright. 'Do you know what Jess told me? . . . He told me that Christina reckoned he was the father of the child she was carrying.'

'That's why he gave her money – to get shot of her?'

'Didn't occur to me at the time. I thought it was to do with that drug deal they were involved in.'

'Why didn't you tell me?'

There was a strange gleam of neutral vindication in her eyes, like that of a croupier watching the wheel go round for the thousandth time, indifferent to the number and knowing that the house will prevail regardless of where the balls come to rest. She wiped something from her face and resumed her static stare: 'You can answer that yourself.'

He locked up the flat, pocketed the keys. They took the lift down to the gelid spaces of Atlantic Wharf and walked in silence along East Canal Wharf. The last of the light streamed along its deadwater, some odd, paranoiac laughter in the soft reflections.

When they reached his flat, the door was ajar. He'd forgotten to double lock. It had been the easiest of break-ins. Farissey went ahead to check for intruders. Two minutes later, he called Victoria up.

A charred playpen had been placed in the middle of the room. His father's pictures had been removed from their glass frames. Long knife slashes went through the boxers' torsos. Overturned files and papers were scattered on the floor. The boxes of drugs were untouched: Jess knew that Farissey stored only over-the-counter products in the flat.

Victoria got to her knees, went through loose papers and files. 'He's taken all the documents relating to the trial,' she said. 'Probably worried we'll pass them on.'

'What documents? I thought they were all lodged at the solicitors' office.'

'I took two copies of everything relating to you, Jess and JD,' she said. 'For my own use. I didn't want to do that kind of thinking in work.' She took a cigarette – her first in months – from his packet of Park Drive; dragged on it with an expression of appalled relish. 'What do you reckon Jess'll do with the documents?'

He didn't answer, but drew on his own cigarette, stood stock-still. She talked on, describing how the documents comprised interviews, hypotheses, hypnosis transcripts. But he wasn't thinking about the trial, or about documents. His gaze was fixed on the playpen squatting in the middle of the room; an inert, ugly, primitive and flame-licked piece of carving that had nothing to do with culture, civilisation, *their* life.

Farissey picked up two bottles of stelazine and took off to the nearest pub, the Packet. Sitting alone, before a pint and chaser, his guilt began to rise, take shape.

By shielding Jess from the state, from the psychiatric services, by supplying him with a variety of anti-psychotic drugs, could he have allowed his friend the freedom to realise himself in that ultimate act?

Jess's psyche was tired. A spent-out nature needs greater and greater stimulation. Jess was looking for the ceiling. He wanted to explode out of himself, above himself. Sex wouldn't do it; drugs – mere drugs – wouldn't do it, and Jess didn't have the patience for anything more than cod spirituality. But killing Christina, that might have given him a sense of his own ceiling, his own place, his highest place, where no one and nothing could touch him. Farissey thought of the constant flow of drugs – legal and illegal – between him and Jess, of the dance in which they had spent their days, neither one knowing who was leading whom.

I must get this stelazine to him right now, Farissey thought to himself. Without anti-psychotics, Jess would go up and up. He'd push himself higher, too, with street drugs, and God knows where it would take him. Was Jess sedated when Christina was killed? He was giving Jess the drugs, for sure, but whether he was taking them . . . ? Farissey decided to call a taxi to take him to Jess's mother's house in Canton, but first he had something to check out.

A few minutes later, Pauline Baja opened the door of her council house. Carl was out. 'Doing security work in Newport,' she said. 'Place is full of kids – we've got my sister's lot.'

Standing at the front door, Farissey felt some sweaty dizziness – like the first insinuations of food poisoning – creep up on him. 'We got the gift of a playpen last night.'

'I knows it's not much to look at,' she responded. 'But it all comes in useful.'

'Someone slashed my father's pictures and took some documents.'

'What's a few bits of paper, like? Compared with months in prison waiting trial when you never done nothing?'

There was no malice in her eyes. She looked at him with some sense of a mission all too swifly successful, even with that keen and bewildering disappointment a teenage girl feels on finding that the quested male is all hers before those collusions and staged coincidences can be put into place. Something in Victoria had called to Pauline Baja; some glimpse of another way of living.

At Canton, he waited five minutes for a reply. The weather was strange, folded up, mustering towards a change, a breaking point.

Jess's sister spoke from behind the door chain. 'It's just you, Jack, promise?' Sophie was worried it was a set up. Only an hour ago, a petrol-doused rope had been ignited under the front door of their council house.

'My mother went fucking spare about it; kicked Jess out. Now she's over at my auntie's.'

'Where's Jess gone?'

'Wouldn't say.'

'Not Atlantic Wharf. He dropped his keys round at my place.'

'He could be there. I was with him when he got spares cut.'

'Not much of a hideout, though, is it?' He looked straight into her eyes. Sophie had taken advantage of her mother's absence to attack the spirits cabinet. She wasn't drunk yet, but she wasn't far off either. She had on a lot of garish make-up, a white blouse and black miniskirt. Since she hadn't said anything about going out, Farissey wondered about that five-minute delay at the door. She offered him a smoke. He declined.

'Why did you get into that thing with giving him drugs? You couldn't know what was wrong with him. Why didn't you put a stop to it, let doctors and that look at him?'

'Jess didn't want me to. In any case, he had enough evidence to finish me as a pharmacist.'

She shrugged, draped herself across the armchair. Something seized Farissey just then. He saw her differently; no longer Jess's kid sister, but cruel, shallow, attractive and predatory.

'Any idea where Jess might have gone?' he asked.

'Nope. But he did do something strange before he left.'

Sophie took him to Jess's bedroom. Spray-painted on the wall: TRUTH IS CROOKED, DESTINY A CIRCLE.

'What the fuck that's about, don't ask me,' she said, placing her tumbler on the bedside table. She relit the joint she was smoking.

The room was cluttered with guitars, boxes of sheet music, tapes, records, three guitars propped against the wall. Farissey noticed the packs of tarot cards he'd bought Jess for his sixteenth birthday. Adolescence: that other country. An image drifted into his mind of Jess as a cherub, blocking access to a park or lake or garden.

'C'mon, Jack. Forget about Jess. He's just somebody's brother. Mine, in this case. Leave him and Victoria to their games and their baby.' Her lips twisted around the word 'baby':

Jess's sarcasm frothing around her lips. Something in her tonight, calling to him, in some staveless key.

'If only you'd come along earlier,' she said, pulling herself up on the bed. Her black miniskirt rode above black stockings. That image, chasing him down chasing something out of him. A woman prone, a man stroking her hair: *You don't fuck, don't fuck.*

'Remember when we were teenagers,' she continued. Her face pinched up as she dragged on the roach-end of the joint. Listlessly, she let the roach fall from the bedside. Farissey watched it dying into the carpet.

'I used to say I was on the pill . . . Well, was I fuck? Nothing ever happened, did it? You know why? You don't, do you?'

As she spoke, her eyes misted up, her pupils dilated. Yet there was a strange, wavering and perverse pride in her voice as she revisited, excused and damned her own past. And as she spoke, she transformed herself for him once again. A girl – once more a girl – now on a bed in her mother's house, inviting but vulnerable, a pretty, plump animal. 'C'mon, Jack,' she said more than once as she told her story. For that time, there was nothing in the world he wanted more; nothing in the world he needed less.

'It's not me that you want,' he said, when her story came to a close. There were tears on her face, tears of a sloshed stonehead or tears for a girlself long gone, he couldn't tell.

'Fuck you and fuck you,' she said. 'Get out of this fucking house. I didn't have to tell you all of that.'

Destiny a circle, he thought on the long walk back to Butetown. He tarried around Argyll Square: the last place Christina had been seen. No ghosts of her, no ghosts of Jess. Not even any hustlers out tonight. He walked on, popped his head round the door of Acram's pool hall. Not Jess, not even Jimmy the Hat: just the hall's old, tired, expressionless alsatian returning his stare. Walking straight-backed, slow and pensive towards the iron bridge and the docks, he played over Sophie's story of brother and sister.

She and Jess always did it standing up, her legs hiked around his hips. The tropical fish bore mute witness. There were a few rumours. Perhaps they'd been seen once or twice, although neither brother nor sister could see how – unless someone saw through the street-facing fish tank, through the bubbles and aquatic foliage. Always at the same time: ten in the evening, their mother out to watch their father gig around dismal South Wales venues.

It was just after her fourteenth birthday when they found out. They tried gin and hot baths. He punched her in the stomach a few times: full force, and all. No avail.

Then they saw sense between them, brother and sister. £200: that's what it took, even back in those days. She got a little work in a papershop, and cleaning a B&B in Pontcanna. Jess took on three paper rounds, skipped school to work on a tugboat. On Saturdays, Jess worked as a bookie's runner up in town. Two nights a week, he washed glasses in the House of Blazes. His life was a flurry, a commitment, a mission. For once Jess hadn't felt, felt something like peace. From his school, there came threats of expulsion. He aped the role of a teenage rebel to the hilt. On the tugboats, he picked up dope and some speed. He brazened it out with school and parents for the twelve weeks it took to raise the money. She was twenty-five weeks gone when the backstreet doctor operated in Newport. Labour was induced, the foetus killed. That was why, she knew now, she'd never conceived in twenty years of trying.

Destiny a circle. At 10.30, he tarried in Loudoun Square. He stood awhile amid the tower blocks on what was once the site of the House of Blazes: that's where he'd met Jess first, all those years ago. Could he trust what Sophie – what Jess's sister – had just said? True, she wanted to set him off against Jess, against Victoria. But her story had a dark, irresistible logic. All that time in his teens, with Farissey wondering, 'Who was this pregnant girl?' Only for him to know now: 'Why, of course, she was always there, with me, with Jess, with her bedroom beside Jess's bedroom and with every reason herself to keep the secret.'

Loudoun Square was deserted: granite expanses lit up by halogen light. At the late-night grocer, Farissey bought a bottle of whisky. He walked to Angelina Street. He cast an eye down the alleyways near the murder flat; he looked without expectations – Jess was too subtle to set a 'return to the scene of the crime' riddle. The Avondale, further down, offered a better chance.

Truth is crooked. He pondered the first half of Jess's message; took it to signify not just a circular journey but a return to something awry, coiled or deceitful. Perhaps it was bidding him return to the point of the lie, of the primordial lie. Where did the lie start . . . ? In the Avondale that night, as Farissey's memory slipped away from him . . . ?

It was a busy Friday night in the Avondale. He just made last orders. Josie Marshall sat at the counter with a few lesbian friends. She turned her back on him. He couldn't blame her. After all, he'd taken Lida – worse, the baby – out of her life. She was talking about him, he was sure. So when she went out into the corridor, he followed a minute later. Just as he suspected, she was making a payphone call. He finished his drink, debated whether to stay in the relative safety of a public place. He decided against it, followed another intuition, left the pub to walk towards Bute Street.

Across the road from the murder flat, outside the White Hart, he saw Jimmy the Hat standing like a sentinel with his one-piece pool cue in hand. In acknowledgement, Jimmy the Hat raises his cue; cased in steel, it looks like a medieval weapon. Something tugged at Farissey; Jimmy the Hat looked allegorical, a dream figure in the light haze that had fallen over the bay.

Farissey sidled up to him. 'You seen Jess?'

'Me, I'm not saying nothing.' For once, Jimmy the Hat looked grave. 'Tag along if you want to see something.'

Farissey walked with Jimmy the Hat as he bought a kebab. Resting his cue, Jimmy tore the kebab in half.

Passing under the Bute Street Bridge, they encountered an old greybeard dosser, dancing to some imagined music. 'Used to be a rear gunner,' he said.

Farissey passed over a fistful of coins, looked over this ruin of a man: broad-shouldered and imponderable against the scant streetlighting. The dosser reached into his pocket and offered a large piece of unwrapped cheese.

'I shouldn't give any away really,' said the dosser. 'It's for my friends. I cuts it into tiny pieces for them and puts the pieces all over my body at night.'

'Who are your friends?' Jimmy the Hat smiled.

'The rats. They keeps me warm at night – like a blanket.'

A few minutes later they reached Sven Books. Jimmy opened the front door. Farissey looked at the display of newspapers, pool cues, cue extensions, green and blue chalk, dartboards, boards for backgammon and chess. Jimmy the Hat took a swift inventory, turned off the light. He then lit up the backroom, retreated upstairs.

'Thought you were looking when all the time I was drawing you to me.' Jess's voice, Jess's tenor: more throaty, rasping than usual.

Can't lead a chase without being chased yourself, Farissey reflected as he pushed through the plastic curtains. Two hard chairs at the centre of the back room. He took the other.

'What a setup. Worked a real beaut', this one.' Jess was drinking cheap red wine from the bottle. He was smug and invulnerable, like a man in a waking sleep. His eyes were lidded, his face puffy and pale but for a beaded alcohol flush. He was wearing a white Mexican wedding shirt and formal black trousers with a sharp crease. Beside him was the grey holdall that he carried with him everywhere of late.

Eyes of models, at every corner of the room, models that looked no different from the ones he'd seen that Easter Sunday morning, as he awoke beside Jess on a plastic sheet, blood on his clothes, his mind blank. Blackness now beyond the plastic curtain where before crisp dawn had intruded in thin, accusatory shafts. The two blonde girls on the cover of *Janus*; back to back, their eyes trained on some unimaginable horizon . . .

When Farissey told of the break-in at the flat, Jess drummed his fingers on the side of his chair. 'We're in it now. Primo comes up to me tonight and says: "we're gonna make a new pussy hole for you." "Fuck you too," I say. "I'm fine." Course I'm feeling good at the time. On a few things tonight. Up and down like a fucking fiddler's elbow.'

Farissey passed across a bottle of stelazine. Indifferently, Jess put the bottle in his trouser pocket.

'Got any coke, Jess?'

Jess reached for his drugs-case, some childish buoyancy about him now. 'Pink flecks – the best, man. See how generous your Jess is. Or maybe he isn't. We got things to talk about, Black Jack. See, you've made that girl your own when the fucking deal was we carve her up – right down the middle.' He repeated 'carve her up' with a high-pitched giggle. He inhaled smoke, puffed out his brawny chest from his shirt. His eyes, though, were steady, depthless. 'Halfway, right up the middle. One bit for you, one for me.'

'Victoria wouldn't spit at you. What was the idea behind that condom stunt, anyway?'

'Carve her up,' Jess continued. 'Like the other one.'

Jess laughed: *laughing mouths that disgorged police sirens.* Mockery then Farissey saw in countless, computeless eyes of porn models: 'Let me suck your soul into my image,' those eyes said.

'You ever get dreams or images with a face spewing laughter?' asked Farissey.

'A clown or dwarf in them? A clown vomiting minestrone into a bowl?'

'Nah – because I know what it is.' Jess smiled. His smile was broad, venal, lopsided.

'What?'

'The faggot who lived above the murder flat, the one they call Midge. He saw it, smelled it. He was on the staircase, catching puke in his hands in case any spilled.'

'A guy on the floor with her? She's in a heap? A guy stroking her hair? The guy saying, "You don't fuck, you don't fuck"?'

'Stroking's halfway there, Jack.' Jess sipped on the wine bottle, winced with the distaste of a man in need of more concentrated liquor. 'In and out of her ear; something finer, so fucking crisp and fine because she don't fuck. See, I've given her money; she pretends to go to London, turns back. Then, I see the light on the window and the curtains drawn – that's the code she gives to Lida to let her know whether she's asleep, just hanging around or "entertaining". So when I come on to Christina like a punter – well, she can't say much in that case, 'cause it's business. And what's she take me for? A fucking punter? That's what I'm asking myself when she takes her jacket off. Well, she doesn't fuck with me, doesn't even respond just then.'

Farissey took a sip from the wine bottle. His eyes roved the shelves. A contact magazine called *New Directions* sprang out of the run: a sallow, thirtysomething woman on its cover; her flesh loosehanging, sloughing off with swansong invite. A world on a plane, in one dimension: false images thou shalt not worship.

Farissey gathered himself to speak. 'How about a scarecrow shaking blood from its tattered coat?'

'Mr X, Jack, man. Mr X is as skinny as fuck, with lank, greasy hair, a frayed black duffel coat. A punter, I suppose. Comes up, catches me off-guard, gets the knife but then has a go at you. That revives you. And you're both wrestling around. But there's pools of her blood, see, and streaks on the walls. In fact, it's amazing you don't get more blood on you. Anyway, I pull him off you, and you get up, and he's got the knife, and he backs off on to the landing and you don't kick him exactly. More like you push him in the chest with your foot down the stairs only for the fucker to take a lucky tumble against the door and get out, like, I don't know . . .'

A shock into the night. That phrase bubbling up from Farissey's dark spaces.

'JD comes up then. He's seen Mr X and seen the knife, but Mr X is faster along the street outside. JD comes into the room, says he'll bring the van and block the view of the entrance. Wait inside the door, wait to hear two beeps.'

'And Carl Baja?'

'Way, way further down Angelina Street. Doesn't notice a thing. See, these two prosties are still catting up to each other and the Idren are howling about drug money.'

'And you and me, walking round wire-meshed buildings, the Mardy rubbish tip?'

'You're on your own trip there,' Jess said. He became thoughtful. 'Unless you're thinking of when we were kids and we ambushed that woman in the industrial clearing down at the Dumballs Road. Mardy's kind of the same. We feel up her tits and you panic and say we should let her go.'

A shameful, repressed moment from Farissey's early teens catching up with him, grafting itself on to Christina's murder. A woman in his eyes, then: maybe twenty, like Christina. The ghost of a girl now recalled amid the looming magazines . . .

'And what did you Mickey Finn me with?'

'Midis, midis, lots of midis. Saved them for a few girls I know, but then I get this idea.'

Midazolam: the date-rape drug. Causes confusion and memory loss, especially in combination with alcohol. Can induce a waking sleep.

'Also some grievous bodily harm.'

GHB: gamma hydroxybutyrate acid, a cruder amnesiac.

'Had to give you a huge spike because you had buckets of speed in you.'

Enough speed for the flickers to make an imprint: shadows across a blank screen.

'Turned the tables that, didn't it? I was going to leave you there, knife by your side. A real fucking pigeon, you of all. Could've made me proud, that, but then Mr X stumbles up and everything's gone to fuck. But I was glad later. Because I couldn't have done that to you. I know that now. I'd have had to confess myself, or at least make that we both did her.'

'And why are you confessing now?'

'Who's confessing? And who's confessing to who? I could always say the same in reverse. *In reverse*, Jack. Given what you said under hypno, they'd build a stronger case against you than me. Every time, Black Jack. Didn't tell you that, did I? That hypnosis thing. I didn't go down. Kept myself above it: didn't give the police an iota.'

Jess patted the holdall at his side. Farissey noticed that a strap was discreetly wound around Jess's upper arm. It was entwined in a raffish yellow scarf. Jess's smart gaberdine was neatly folded over the back of the chair.

'Outsmarted you, Jack. Like I did in India. In Benares. Couldn't get off the morphine, could you? Remember that Indian civil servant, one who takes to you on account of him having been educated by the Christian brothers. Used to go on about "errant cats and vagabond dogs"? So he gets you all this whisky and you're drinking night and day, and still the morphine cravings are at you. There's you thinking you can get off anything but the booze. So why isn't it working? Well, Jack . . . I was injecting morphine in your calves when you were asleep. I was . . . *jacking* you up.' Jess laughed the same chattering laugh.

Farissey felt like ripping Jess's tongue out; felt numbness in his own tongue. 'I worked that one out. That's why I packed up and went to the other side of town. I even came back to get you, organised all the travel back to Britain, medicated you when you came off the morphine.'

'I owe you, Jack man, Jack-in-the-box. Don't ever think I don't.' Jess stumbled over his words. Tears ran down his cheeks.

'JD's in intensive care,' Jess continued. 'The Big Man done because of those fucking documents. What's Victoria thinking about, the stupid cow? Keeping those things in your flat?'

Trying to think of everything, Farissey had forgotten about JD. 'Which hospital?'

'What's it matter? JD's done for. Way to remember him is this . . . See, Jack, we're going to do something that'll make our lives a whole lot easier.'

'Like what, precisely?'

'Precisely: we're going to kill Carl Baja. Like he's just about killed JD.'

'*Us* kill *Carl?*' Farissey asked before realising he was asking. He went quiet for a minute. 'Us kill Carl with what? Our bare hands?'

'Knives, man. Poetic fucking justice.'

'It could just happen . . .' *It could: just now.* 'On condition we drink this bottle of whisky to it.' Jess shook on the deal, held Farissey's hand for much longer than was decent: something spongy, springing, soft in Jess's grip.

Jess threw off close on a gill, rested his head, sighed. For twenty minutes, he listed various injustices – spanning a quarter of a century – they'd suffered at Carl Baja's hands. Listening with feigned outrage, Farissey passed back the bottle.

Jess slowed down. His words were damp, dredged up like decaying foliage from a river bed. 'He works the Casa, man . . . Four o'clock Sunday morning he goes to get his fucking newspaper . . . On the Dumballs Road, the warehouse . . . that's where . . .'

Jess's eyes lidded as gulp by gulp they killed the bottle. Jess went silent. Light rain outside; light itself coming through the shutters. Farissey welcomed the rain, wished it was inside the back room itself, washing away the images, unsullying so many girls, way, way too many of them. Watching the beads of rain form into silvery shivers on the window, he knew he had to empty himself of pathos. He had been in that murder room. He and Jess had emerged from that room as if from the same body . . .

That other body? Was it dead asleep now? That other body became another body: Jimmy the Hat silhouetted behind the plastic curtain. Barefoot, he slipped in, squeezed Jess's wrist, sent a wave of Zippo flame over the back of Jess's hand. He eased the strap of the holdall away from that body.

'I heard everything,' Jimmy said. 'Sift through his bag. I'm kicking the fucker out sharpish tomorrow.'

Shirts, socks, plectrums, a razor, shaving foam, empty drug cases. Farissey filched a diary and a tape.

'True about JD?'

'C.R.I.'

The Cardiff Royal Infirmary. Ten minutes away.

'Give my whatever to Dolores,' Jimmy the Hat said.

As Farissey walked around the prison and towards the Cardiff Royal Infirmary, he heard ambulance sirens in the background.

JD probably wired in a bed, Jess comatose in Sven Books, Carl Baja perhaps doing a last line of coke. How little this world values light and life; how little he values . . .

Another set of sirens started up. He didn't look back. He looked to the heavens so as not to look at the dark masonry of the hospital, felt as though the sky described a dome as he walked through a city of glass.

Chapter Thirteen

JD had suffered two coronaries, internal bleeding, broken ribs, bruising to his kidneys and damage to his sternum. It was too soon to say what sort of chances he had. He'd been talking about an Enfield .303 and a girl dead on the kitchen floor. His Korean rifle, Farissey thought. He's compressed the two great losses of his life into a single figure. Farissey remembered JD's words as they drove from the back room of Sven Books to Windsor Esplanade. *Another young girl dead, without rhyme or reason.*

JD had been found on the Tremorfa Industrial Estate. A print factory owner had heard a report of a burst water main. He saw the blue transit in the little alley formed by the two factories. JD was lying among foliage, briar, pebbles and rough stone. In the car, JD recovered some lucidity. The Baja brothers had ambushed him outside the Schooner pub. They stole his wallet, forced him to drive down to Seawall Road. There they kicked and punched him around in the back of the van.

It was mid-morning when Loudon Hargest turned up at the hospital. He wore a black shirt and grey sports jacket. His face was bloated, puce. He was having problems in his marriage, eating alone late at night. He'd been seen throwing up under the table in a Butetown curryhouse.

Hargest asked how much money JD carried around with him. 'A couple of thousand, at least,' Farissey estimated. 'Comes in useful for backhanders in the building trade. You know how it works.'

'This wasn't anything to do with me,' said Hargest to Dolores. 'I kept you all off the witness stand.'

'We know that,' said Dolores, tolerantly. 'But then who, and – how – ?'

Those documents, Farissey knew. Carl and Pauline Baja: *that charred playpen.*

It wasn't quite noon when Farissey got out of the CRI. At 11.30, he'd stood in the hospital courtyard as Dolores talked of how a heart attack is more painful than giving birth. 'Waves of pain, you feel. You just give yourself up to the pain. And then the weird thing: you forget. That makes women go through it again and again, go back to men against all good sense.'

Farissey walked through Adamsdown to the town centre. As he walked he wondered what state of health Dolores was in herself to be talking like that. A looking back which is really a looking forward, a rehearsal and prophesy that the will is receding and you are readying yourself to die, that you are going over and back or wherever it is you go. Something had passed between them in that courtyard. Another light; some poisonous orange iridescence.

At Bute Street, he phoned Victoria. She was in work, sorting out the last details of her maternity leave.

'Whatever you do, don't mention the documents to Dolores. She's looking for someone to blame and—'

'I've got to tell her,' she said. Her voice smalled off. 'Maybe it's my fault.'

'It's not. It's the Baja's fault. It's partly my fault. Mostly, it's—'

He'd intended to say 'Jess's fault' but stopped himself. As he walked down Bute Street, he couldn't recall what he'd said.

Something like 'the universe's fault, the fault of evil in the first place'.

He paused at Loudoun Square. He remembered when Bute Street was one continuous drag and the North and South Wales Inn stood at its centre. Back then it was known to all and sundry as the Blood Kitchen in honour of the days when Jimmy Driscoll sparred with his shadow in its basement.

Turning into Alice Street, he remembered when it was Peel Street and the House of Blazes stood at its centre. He thought back to serving at that bar throughout his teens, relieving his mother's stints with the father now dead. He thought of those teenage seances he presided over, of those ragged letters and the YES and NO at the poles. He recalled that unearthly, wicked thrill, picked up by the pet labrador who quaked in the next room, curled for its life under the small dining table. 'Let's go straight to the devil,' Farissey said one afternoon. 'It's an experiment. If we can prove the existence of absolute evil, then we can infer the existence of absolute good.'

What did the existence of absolute evil mean, Farissey asked as he walked in the shadow of the tower blocks towards Louisa Street. He lit another cigarette. The afternoon was windy, the down draught from the tower blocks colossal: ideal conditions for relishing strong tobacco, the air helping the smoke get deeper into his lungs.

At the Loudoun Square grocer's he bought two and a half bottles of vodka and five packets of Park Drive on a cheque. In the flat, he showered, changed clothes. He poured himself five measures of vodka, leafed through Jess's diary. Song lyrics, pages of stonehead philosophising, drawings of seahorses, amoeba and foetuses sat beside intermittent diary entries. On one page Jess had quoted from the Second Book of Samuel: 'I am distressed for thee, my brother: very pleasant hast thou been unto me: thy love for me was wonderful, passing the love of women.' On the top of the page was an aphorism from Nietzsche's *Beyond Good and Evil*: 'He who fights with monsters should look to it that he does not become a monster. And when

you gaze too long into an abyss, the abyss also gazes into you.'
Farissey checked the entries for April.

3rd April: Christina won't lay off this idea that I'm the
father. Says Tony takes her up the shitter. Uses condoms
with everyone else – so she says!
Holy Thursday: Jess thinks ahead. Sell my acoustic Gibson
for £280. Lay the plan with her. She'll get her money when
I see her get on the train. With the £500 she's conned from
the Bajas, there's plenty left over to get herself settled and
get the thing aborted.
Easter Saturday: 3 p.m. Jack pissed up in the Packet. I
move quickly. Help Tina pack. Got her to station for the
4.25. Won't see that piece of meat again.

At the foot of that page, he'd scrawled: 'Truth is crooked,
destiny a circle (Nietzsche: *Zarathustra*).' Again Farissey felt his
own complicity. All those years he'd passed on snippets of
wisdom to Jess without providing contexts. It was like putting a
sword in the hands of a child.

Farissey put on the tape. It was a kind of guitar symphony
Jess had made using multi-tracking. It paid subdued homage to
the Grateful Dead's 'Dark Star'. Jess's voice started up. He
wasn't singing but declaiming. The guitars went into a lull,
lapped invitingly around his voice.

*'To turn his own trick with this filth and take its returns, yes,
never ending where it never started, playing itself out infinitely, only
so much time in which to shift to another story, huddled for mercy on
the floor, now wringing the blood from his hands – wanting the
blood? – that being the last he had of her, like it was fixed and
nothing in that room would ever change again, spotted or flecked
ceiling, blood of walls, hers, condoms open but unused, ashtray, bulb
naked – seeing – couldn't look too long at – taping or ticking silver
thread shot through the flesh, what was that? Solely dreamed of that,
dreamed of a child – 'Wasn't our little girl any more' – driven down
the dark shafts, a place begone, like nothing on earth, not a word nor
a picture to fit. 'Have I lost you when I'm so full to bursting with the*

emptying of you? Have I lost you altogether, in this wrenching, in this blood?' The door burst wide at the very point of breath. Would've been a girl, he thinks, he knows, and running her eyes along the knife, the fingers, the hand, to a face, wet with tears, frozen in frenzy, pushing itself into trance, calling some other power to act. 'It's not me; it's not you', saying something, maybe sobbing, 'Forgive me, I'm sorry'. She thinks he must be going for her groin but if he is he just keeps missing. Out of puddles eyes stare, funny, how sticky, how warm, you wouldn't think, all those loving faces, her mother, lost, like her child could keep her, this love, like drowning, kind and helpless now, that's when the cutting starts, the pain hits, God above, from the inside out, a goose walking over your grave, like nothing you'd ever feel, fingernails ripped, close to the bone, whirling now, losing it, another world as he presses one hand hard into her face, holding it with fingers, thin, so strong, and he grasps her hair and twists her around; velvet and sort of electric, and her head shocked like light flooding along the canal, calm, eerie sheen, and she wonders how it could be so bright out there and she feels like she's in a cage and wants to claw or scratch her way out but she's just pawing; so cold, a scalpel nearly, and where'd he get it from? Hadn't seen anything when he comes in and she makes for the window, gets there long enough to see that it's blue, like the streets and the sky were bruised. There was all this hell to pay in the street, scared of it as she was, then shouting, arguing, the usual hustles, deals or pimps and hustlers, and she wished she was there in the thick of things. There was the sound of cars in the background and she's wondering too why'd she ever let him back, when she felt something coming on like this, why she always drew the worst, kept returning to it and she knew it was over for good and it's all too much to bear losing blood as she was like he wanted to take her but then some she'd seen that look before but hadn't realised what it meant until now: so clinical as well, dear God, so far gone and he's not himself, the strength, running up through his arms, it's all electricity, his face, sweating, throbbing, as he comes at her again looking as he did, she knew that the only sacred and defended space that was for ever her own would be hers no longer. And at that moment she knew she'd never be a mother.'

His mind went back to those adolescent days when Jess tried to fold their voices into one. He thought of Jess's interest in the cut-up method of lyric writing, in montage. Why does he want so meticulously to reverse the movement of my hypnosis-speak? Farissey wondered. Given the time taken, Jess might as well have created new and more malign juxtapositions. What was Jess trying to tell him? What was his secret self – his better self – trying to communicate?

A dry-mouthed weariness came over Farissey. There was some muted voice at him like the one in the ears of a gambler throwing good money after bad, the one voice he doesn't want to hear. 'Cease,' the voice said. 'Cease,' it said, softer and softer.

He phoned the Central Police Station. A sergeant suggested he deposit the tape and diary at the desk. Farissey insisted on being put through to Loudon Hargest. He sat back in his armchair. Some image of the murder began to form in his mind; some twenty rings later he fell asleep holding the long, seemingly interminable line to Loudon Hargest.

He fell straight into dream. In the first, he was on some dry plain, morning and evening stars the same: seeing past and future, end and beginning, good and evil in a single instant that didn't happen in time at all. A bunch of bridal dresses that were also cot linings and hospital sheets, and a body wrapped in bandages that he had to unbandage; unwinding until he realises with horror that the body was no more than the bandages in which it was wound.

In the second, he was running through dark-glass streets that narrowed and opened on to incandescent squares. A car pulled up beside him with sawn-off shotguns pointed at the windscreen. Carl Baja was hovering over the town like an eagle menacing coots. A fire started up in a square. A Sikh was breathing flame, his digestive tract having been filled with petrol. The fear abated. The Baja-eagle became a dove, and he and Carl were kids again and sole mourners along the Catholic aisles of reconciliation, rapt before the absent place of a deadly, mastering, pneumonic paternity. A church bell rang in his ears until, through the muzzles of awakening, he recognised the insistent ringing of his doorbell.

He moved cautiously to the window. A drowsed mulatto, one Farissey didn't recognise; weary, almost reluctant, his finger taut on the doorbell. Farissey took a hefty draught of vodka, removed the ring and watch that had belonged to his father and placed them in a drawer in the living room. He remembered a half-bottle of vodka in the kitchen. Through the window, he saw Tony Baja lounging at the fire exit. No surprises there; all exits covered. He pulled his crombie out of the bedroom wardrobe, slipped the vodka into its inside pocket. He locked the door behind him, posted his keys through the letterbox, heard them fall with a chime of finality.

The mulatto was now in the driver's seat; Carl Baja in the back. Farissey ambled to the car, clipped his cigarette on the wing mirror. Tony Baja got in last, placed cigarettes and lighter on the dashboard.

'Hello, Carl,' Farissey says, arranging himself in the back, beside his old schoolmate.

Carl Baja nodded silently. His eyes darted left and right in a face that was otherwise ponderous, marble-smooth.

'Where we going?' Farissey asked.

'Across the Severn Bridge,' Carl said. 'But not just yet.' Five minutes, they waited for Tony. He got into the passenger seat reluctantly, as though it were a cage.

The car drove out of Butetown, pulled up outside the Triad Centre next to the railway station.

'Those builders, they certainly fucking carry,' Carl Baja said. He pulled a massive roll of notes from the inside pocket of his leather jacket. 'Three and a half grand for less than an hour's work.' He put the roll back into his pocket, drew out three credit cards. 'John Vincent Dwyer', he read. 'You seen him?'

'No, not today. I've been working,' Farissey lied. Live credit cards, he thought. The only trace or trail . . .

'Sell the cards. Ask for £50, settle for £20,' Carl said to his younger brother. 'Make like we're doing them a favour.'

Carl Baja grinned, looking at Farissey for approbation of his cunning. Farissey shrugs, ignores Baja, watches Tony gain access to the centre. Torturing Triad eyes, looking down on us, Farissey wonders.

'All right, start thinking like why you puts us on Angelina Street that night,' Carl Baja says, craning around to look through the rear window for whatever vain furies might be witlessly in pursuit. 'Start thinking, Mr John "Jack" Farissey,' he says, cutting the syllables of a surname like a pick breaks ice.

'First interview,' Farissey says, 'I say you weren't there. By the second I know that they've got shedloads of other people saying you were. I even told Loudon Hargest that you two wouldn't – couldn't – have done it.'

'Cut it,' Carl Baja says. 'You knows that shit don't count for nothing. I read the interviews.'

Silence as they wait and watch the Triad door. Farissey looks at the Chinese characters it bore. Someone had once translated them for him; he can't remember how.

'How did you manage to fuck up, Tone, you fucking empty-head?' Carl asks as Tony comes back with JD's credit cards unsold.

'Me? Me fuck up? Those Chinks are streets ahead of you every time. They knows from the start it was a setup. Then they tells me JD is in intensive care and I'll be joining him.'

'What the fuck! They don't hardly even know JD,' Carl said. 'And you falls for that!' Carl Baja paused. A look of intelligent desperation passed across his face. 'What's he in intensive for?'

'Massive heart attack, that's what they says.'

Relief flooded Carl Baja's face. 'A man his age, no telling when he's going to go. Fold up any time, they do. Me, I've got the heart of a lion.'

Baja emptied a packet of Benson and Hedges, arranged the loose cigarettes in his jacket pocket. He tore the credit cards, put them into the empty cigarette box. The car pulled up by a litter bin. Tony Baja got out and dropped the crushed packet into the bin. Next day, that bin would be emptied and nothing but word of mouth would connect the Bajas to JD's coronary.

The car spun around the station forecourt, turned from Wood

Street to St Mary's Street. Carl told the mulatto driver to speed up as the road curled around the prison wall. As they joined the M4, Tony seemed to be asleep in the front. Either that or unusually still.

'Slow down here, bra',' Baja instructed the driver as they passed Llanwern Steelworks, once the great engine of industrial South Wales.

'My old man worked there,' Baja said, a strangely lyrical mood stealing up on him. 'Built the Severn Bridge. Used to take me to look at all the millions of cars going over it. Your old man wasn't shit beside mine. What did he do? Pull pints and piss up the profits. There's work in that steel game, spar. A man's work.'

'My old man and yours, they got on all right,' Farissey said, remembering the school rugby team and how Old Baja would shout and swear – all gravel and wheeze and fiery effort – to fuck him up real good if he missed a conversion. A forty-year-old West Indian standing on a rugby touchline chain-smoking Woodbines into his remaining lung, and breathing dread and curse and threat into a teenager's Saturday morning.

'Your dad was the only fucking Paddy my old man had a good word to say about.'

'And they died within a month of each other,' Farissey said. With one lung removed, Baja's father smoked himself to death; Farissey's father continued drinking after cirrhosis was diagnosed. Nearly a quarter of a century ago: puberty and the death of the father.

'God rest their souls,' Farissey continued. 'And what do we learn? Where have we come? Out in this car with your lieutenants in front.'

'That's my father you talking about, too,' Tony Baja said. He cut a couple of lines of coke on a pocket mirror.

'Let's have everyone dead, Carl, like our dads are dead. Why not? Why don't we just do that?' Farissey spoke with calculated passion, following the flow of his recent dream like a bicycle downhill, a lover the descent into post-coital reverie.

'Man, I don't want no one dead,' Carl Baja said airily, relishing the coke lift. 'Me, I'm a peacekeeper. You finds me that prostitute, Lida, and nothing happens. Not to you, anyway. Where is she?'

'St Paul's, I imagine. I never knew Bristol that well.'

'Don't look so worried,' Carl said. 'We won't put a mark on you.' Tony Baja laughed maniacally. The mulatto joined in; nervous, anxious to conform. 'Three and a half grand, man,' Carl continues. 'So I'm giving out presents.'

It was hustling time in St Paul's. Eight o'clock and a blustery September evening: the sky rainy and darkness fallen like brocade. The grand old houses had been rented into decline. Just like Butetown when he and Baja were boys, Farissey remarked. Baja nodded with an odd pursed grin.

The car pulled up alongside every streetwalker. A wig-big blonde, flaring in the hips, shimmied her arse at the car. She squeezed up to Tony, pulled her skirt to reveal see-through knickers. Tony wants to get involved, Farissey can tell.

'We don't want to do none of that fucking business with you,' Carl said. The girl looked in agate terror at Carl Baja. She doesn't know any Lida, but said that the newer girls did business on the edge of the pitches.

The car crawled a side-road just outside the red-light area. A row of tired-looking pretties were posturing against glistening house-railings.

'What do you want me here for anyway?' Farissey asked, as Lida's ghostly face jumped out of the railings at him. Did anything betray his response? He couldn't tell. 'You saw plenty of her at the trial,' he said, remembering that Tony himself had a little thing going with Lida in any case.

'That ain't the only reason we've taken you out.'

Lida had dyed her hair platinum blonde. She was wearing a smart miniskirt with knee-high white boots. No mascara now but sloshes of suntan paint. She had given herself away to Farissey only by her nervy, girlish habit of flicking hair away from her face.

She's a mother, Farissey thought. *Me, I'm not any kind of a thing, really.*

'Not that one either,' Farissey said.

Carl Baja sensed some hesitation in his tones. The tension in the car was building. It wasn't all emanating from Farissey.

Carl Baja lit a cigarette, looked at Lida with sharkish eyes; looked for that part of a soul that must disclose itself, face the worst, know that there is no worse to come.

'No – that ain't her, Carl,' Tony says, to Farissey's astonishment. 'Ain't her – no way.' Tony must then have seen through it too. This was his ex-lover and once his coke line. This was the girl who gave him up to the police, accused him of murder from the witness stand.

'No way,' Farissey says, realising he's along as a second witness. Carl would have him down as too survivalistic to take a beating to shield Lida. Through Farissey, Carl Baja could pinpoint disloyalty on his brother's part. Within this weird triangle, Lida slipped out of the picture.

After another half-hour of incoherent shakedowns, Carl Baja accepted the futility of his mission. They drove in total silence, on the M32 to the M4, over the Severn Bridge and beyond Chepstow.

In that silence, Farissey realised that Tony Baja must be the father of Lida's child. What sort of man jeopardises the mother of his child? His hypnosis-speak came to mind. Christina: '*And then she knew she'd never be a mother.*' Where Farissey had started the narrative, Jess had ended it. Demothering – his first thought, Jess's last. Jess had reversed the order of that hypnosis session. Why? Well, he wasn't just recalling an event in the past. He was also projecting one into the future. Murder lay ahead as well as behind. That stuff about doing in Carl Baja was pure misdirection.

'Just listen for a second, Carl. Do what you like to me. But get Jess first. Hundred per cent he killed Christina. Ninety-nine per cent he's going to do something terrible next.'

Carl Baja looked directly into Farissey's eyes as though hoping to scorch a hole in that glassy, burnished melancholy behind which a score of tangled tendernesses, fears and traumas had been impacted, cankered.

'I fucking hates that. Don't you, Tone? Trying to save your own skin by dropping your mate in the shit. I fucking hates that. I thought you was braver than that, Jack.'

Tony turned around in the passenger seat. The tip of a lighted joint held to Farissey's eyes. 'Dug a fucking grave for yourself there. Dug it good and deep.' His voice spiralled up hysterically. He has his part to play, Farissey reflected morosely. If only he could be in Tony's place now.

Back in Cardiff, Baja insisted they take the slower route to the docks, over Tremorfa Bridge and on to the industrialised marshlands of Rover Way. The small red car pulled up on to one of the loading ramps of the small neighbouring factories.

'See that sky? See these buildings? There ain't nothing of it going to look the same to you again.'

Not a soul in sight and just the waiting now. A gun? A knife? Not a mark, Baja said. Suffocation?

'Picnic time,' the mulatto giggled, high-pitched and girlish, as he opened the glove compartment and passed something back to Carl Baja.

'Open your fucking mouth, Jack man.'

'Fucking waste,' Tony said. 'Why don't we just rip his fucking liver out? Least we gets to enjoy the damage.'

'Don't be a fucking tight cunt, Tony. Three and a half grand to the good and you're thinking peanuts. Chinese torture – string it out. And you say those fucking Chinks are ahead of me.'

Baja pushed Farissey's lips as far apart as they could go without splitting and eased fingers like sledges into the back of his throat. Farissey felt tiny things flutter down his throat. Insects? Butterflies? The thought was too absurd. Baja was putting butterflies into Farissey's stomach? As though the metaphorical ones needed their lepidopteran counterparts? Farissey would have laughed but that he was half-choking.

'Sit fucking still.' Baja pushed Farissey's neck back for some five minutes. Tony Baja let out a strange hiss of breath. The mulatto began humming 'Picture yourself on a boat on a river . . .'.

'There isn't nothing going to look like nothing again, spar.'

And then Farissey knew what Carl Baja meant; knew it in his own words, his own dreads. 'Not a mark on you.' Unwritten histories, like the sulphur nightly scraped under toenails by clever spouse killers; characters for ever lost by a computer.

Baja would hear of him destitute, wandering, in and out of curfew, counselling and asylum; wide-eyed, fearful and deranged and looking like a century's horrors had been grafted on to his synapses. No one would ever think to ask how Farissey got like that. They'd all put it down to fate, or the curious interplay of genes, bad stock. Because, well, that's what it was, wasn't it? The right man bred to await the wrong time. It couldn't be any other way now, could it, spar? Just because someone down here is pulling the strings don't mean to say it's not destiny, do it?

It would be like taking the road to Damascus backwards, a dawn recomposed by the building, brewing night. To never see in skies anything but imprecations and treachery, or hear the chatter of birds without hearing also a whirring fury of omens in his own head. He would burn on and out, burn in the single hope that these electric storms of Christ and Kali be finally quelled, the dramas come to fruition on a birthday, an intersection of roads, or a car's iconic numberplate and himself then be gone, buried, drowned, whatever, and vindicated.

Farissey would never know how much acid Carl Baja forced into him that night.

Chapter Fourteen

The Bajas kept Farissey with them for three-quarters of an hour to prevent him from regurgitating the acid. He was just getting the first trippy intimations – raindrops on the windscreen looking like pearls or magic bubbles – when they pushed him out of the car and on to Rover Way. Sitting on the wasteground, he checked his watch. It was just after eleven. The very worst should be over by eight or nine in the morning, he told himself. He clung to one word, one concept that would elude him when the acid came through: *time*. Time ticked off the ledger of experience. Mechanical time, not the indivisible time of dream or pleasure or hell.

Farissey recalled the bad trips he'd experienced. The evil genius of acid was its power to persuade you that there was no self before the drug, no self or homecoming afterwards or even the bleak certainty of a paracetamol suicide who knows that he or she has chosen to die, despite that choice having been made in another order of being, by a self now strange.

He took the half-bottle of vodka out of his crombie, lost himself awhile in contemplation of the colourful label and the picture of a Cossack which he first found funny and then disturbing – as though it, too, had eyes, eyes that were on him. He sipped from the bottle, gave himself over to the sky.

The evening was heavy, hanging, like Cardiff was shrouded by a dirty shawl. He imagined all the birds nesting in the sky, as if the legion crows gave to night its quality not of darkness but occluded light. He looked at the skies as if at a dark, feathery drape. The rain had stopped. He didn't feel cold or wet or hot. He simply didn't feel, not even the trickle of neat vodka down his throat. The headlights of a lorry blinded and then frightened him. He was visible to the road here. He knew that the police must be avoided. Worse to fall apart in a cell than in the threatening and solitary open air.

He moved off Rover Way, saw the marshy land of the Tremorfa foreshore in the distance. He determined to hug the shore, find his way back to Butetown not by road or side-road but by the desolate fields. He thought of alcohol in his flat, heavy downs and antipsychotics in the pharmacy. The pharmacy began to seem like a miasma, something he'd fabricated from an idea. He alternated between walking on air and treading water as he slipped and slid and moaned and laughed and gibbered along the marshy hinterland.

The hard-won estuary provided some consolation. He tried to think of healing water to escape from the mounting pressure inside his head. He sat down awhile, lit a cigarette, became convinced that a great, brooding bird, an osprey perhaps, was lodged in him, slowly unfolding its wings in his skull. He scrambled the banks on the sides of the Clipper Road, still fleeing the bird.

At the Tidal Sidings he began to run, hoping to tire himself and the colonising bird into a peace or lull. He ran swiftly for three-quarters of a mile. He did not stop with any effect of exhaustion: rather he realised that he'd run himself into an impasse between sea and steelworks. He waded ankle-deep through the water. The water didn't feel cold on his legs, just odd: a viscous sensation, almost as though he was walking through treacle. He couldn't register a direction by the moon's borrowed light alone; he simply gave up. He returned to a bank on the shore, gave himself up to the bird in his skull, to the starless night.

He felt some relief when the pressure on his skull lightened – as though the bird had taken wing. Silence lapped around him. He opened his eyes to see a disembodied, bloated and bobbing head. It moved as he moved, stayed exactly at eye level: a big, stupid, childlike and slobbering head. It was not precise in detail: more like an outline or the face on a balloon. He walked back through the docks proper in an effort that seemed like a stone eternity. The walk through those looming, crushing machines, those great heaps of copper and unalloyed metal, coincided with a little shift in the arc of his trip. He knows it later, when he emerges at the eastern border of the docks.

He recoils before the barrier to the docks. Its glass-encased attendants are terrifying, like cave-faces to children, but something in the world outside begins to correspond, albeit ominously, with what he sees, remembers seeing. He flees again, finds marsh space. On the hinterland, he registers the first signs of dawn, realises that night's end does not bring light down to earth from the heavens: rather, light seeps, oozes up from the river, from the grass and concrete, as though it has merely been repressed, vanquished awhile by the sheer heaviness of night. He thinks of light, of natural time, the day that follows night: time he can feed into his head but still incommunicable to his watch.

'Mister! Mister!' he hears. 'Some money for the childer!'

The older of a dozen or so children addressed him from the tinker gates. No more than a child himself but for the treacly and distorted Irish voice as old as penury or its hills. The tinker child was grubby, tousled, wore an adult's jacket. He gestured towards the smaller children, who were scurrying on tractors. The sound of the plastic wheels on gravel was unbearable to Farissey. A dog was growling at dawn in the background; a lorry prowled dockwards like some predatory beast.

Farissey dug into his pocket and flung a fistful of change right at the oldest tinker kid. The whole gaggle scattered like so many pigeons, looking for coins among cars, bits of cars, rusty office chairs and obelisk-like print factory machines ready for the scrapping. The idea came to Farissey just then, like some light fork cutting through his synapses: I have to get home. I have to stop Jess. I have to put myself between him and Victoria. I have to put the shadow of myself between the shadows.

He walked dockwards again, past the graving docks, the transit shed, the King's Wharf and Customs Waterguard. He hoped to walk the poison out of his system. He thought of Sundays, ordinary faraway Sundays that now seemed like idylls, dreams.

As he walks, he feels as if he's walking into facts, events, that somehow exist before we find ourselves in their midst. He thinks of cancer beckoning these cigarettes to our lips, all pulses racing, all clocks ticking in this world splintering back from the millennium – a terminus waiting in all its thunderous and silent banality. He thinks he sees a solitary woman gliding down the shale to the prospectless shore. He distorts her into Napoleon's mother, she who mysteriously took to visiting battlefields long before the emperor was conceived.

He comes to another watery impasse, that small dock known as Dead Man's Point. He looked upwards hoping for some increase in the early light. He feared that nothing was going to break through the sky that hadn't already broken into his own head. The long penance of seagulls started up on the estuary. The sky was pursed up, packed, imploding, singing like his blood, coming out of his head. It felt like an eternity before the sun broke through. The sun pierced that sky like a child's paper sky. It sliced through it like music, in jangles. He waited for some invisible hand to bring the discord to resolution and a long peaceful afternote. This day or dawn or interval between sleeps was the one that counted. Victoria might be awake now on the next fold of the bay: her time just beginning.

Checking his watch again, he sees space, not time, and suspects a trickster god whose watches are in fact maps that offer spiritual navigation to some elect who move undetected in our midst. No sooner does he think 'time' than the hands of his watch start moving backwards. He wonders if 'time' may be taking him back to that moment before the acid was on him.

Might he emerge from this trip backwards? Was he journeying back into the night, and from there to a time before the Bajas got to him? Perhaps his existence might funnel back through that dream of Catholic reconciliation, the reincarnate gangs and those incandescent squares that formed the city of his dreams. Perhaps the trip might ferry him to the forecourt of the Cardiff Royal Infirmary, the church clock striking noon as if for those massed and mighty ranks of the dead of whom the living are but a peculiar, outnumbered species. Perhaps it might carry him over to the time when he phoned Victoria, comforted her like she was his to comfort, or further again, to Friday evening with JD drinking in the Schooner, Farissey preparing dinner and awaiting Victoria's return from work.

But no: that vulnerable light was not day's end, but callous, chattering dawn.

By ten in the morning he'd finally dragged himself into Bute-town. As he walked through mazes of now alien, indecipherable streets, he suspected that his thoughts were being transmitted and transcribed at police headquarters. Voices were saying, 'He's back on Bute Street now', 'He's sat down on a bench', 'He's lighting a cigarette', 'He's outside his flat'.

He fumbled with keys in the lock. The door to the flat wouldn't open. He rang the bell insistently. 'He's not getting an answer,' the voice whispered. 'Where is Victoria?' he asked. 'Staying over with Dolores,' the voice answered.

The voice sounded familiar, mocking. He wondered if Jess was himself at the malignant centre, orchestrating the voices, liaising with police officers.

'He's gone into Val's,' the voice said, flattened out now but pursuant, as if summoning officers. The bistro was quiet, a few solitaries hunched over newspapers like captive, soon-to-spring animals. At the counter he didn't look at Val so much as at some silent, wordless vacancy without images or hue. Then she extruded into his view. A woman grown old. How battle-hardened was her face. It was punctuated by loss, lines curling like commas from her mouth.

'Come in the back, love. You'll feel better there,' Val said. Her words sounded like stones dropped into a hushed lake.

He then apologised vacantly, rambled about the difficulty he had moving from concepts to signs and the impossibility of holding on to the idea for more that a second or so.

He pulled two £10 notes from his pockets and what he thought was a bundle of change. 'A pint of vodka and a pint of tonic,' he said. 'Please bear with me.'

Val came through with the two pint glasses. 'What's going on, Jack?'

'I've been . . .' His teeth chattered; he swayed in the chair. 'Been poisoned . . . Got to drink myself down.' He gulped from one glass, then the other. He did so robotically, with stiff arm movements. He looked around the room. Sun-yellows and sky-blues, untroubled 1950s décor; a sacred heart, a chronological run of family photographs along the mantelpiece.

'Seen Jess?' he asked, his voice alien, resounding like a miracle on the airwaves.

'No, Jack, I don't see Jess for weeks now,' said Val, cagey and distracted. 'But it's funny you should say that. Last night a few of the Idren boys were asking for you and that Jess. I says to them, "I've got enough on my mind anyway".'

The police were trying to close her down on the grounds of drug-dealing on the premises. 'As if a woman my age knows the first thing about drugs.'

'Always rely on your friends for testim . . . you know, support.'

'Friends,' she said, going back into the bistro. 'There are no friends, my friend.'

Alone, his eyes roved around the walls. The birds on the wallpaper jumped out at him. They had messages for him, messages he couldn't decipher. Plovers, oystercatchers, curlews, and birds of prey he couldn't name. In flight, they were the sky's decoration. Fixed, they were primeval, predatory. He thought of those medieval adulteresses tied down in the marketplace for birds to peck at their breasts and stomachs.

He finished the drinks in twenty minutes. He sat smoking as

the pint of vodka began to permeate through the pint of tonic water. His thoughts slowed. He could concentrate a little. He smoked another cigarette. He went to count his money, realised that what lay on the table next to his roll of £10 notes was not change but keys: Jess's spares to Atlantic Wharf, the ones he'd pocketed a couple of days ago. He'd posted his own keys through the letterbox when the Bajas had picked him up. Stop the Bajas stealing them and put out a sign to Victoria, a sign he was gone, against his will.

The thought came to him then – terrible in outline. She went looking for him. She followed the sign. She'd called at Atlantic Wharf. Jess had gone back there. The door rang. Jess had peeped through the judas hole. Wearing a bathrobe or white silk *yukata*, he'd opened the door, smiled that strong-toothed smile, breezily bade her come in as he had done so many times before . . .

On the way to Atlantic Wharf, Farissey picked up a half-bottle of vodka. He sipped on it as he walked towards the anonymous housing complex.

A man on the rack loses consciousness, he thought. Pain closes down his being but not his sense of self. But this anguish belonged less to him than to the air, the ghetto streets of Bute-town, the deadwater of the estuary.

Jack. Jack. Jack Farissey. He repeated the name over and over much as children repeat a proper name, say 'sun' until it becomes hollow, risible, emptied of all fire and fury. Then, he made a mantra of Jess Simmonds, felt its sibilance tear at his nerves. Jess Simmonds. Jack Farissey. Farissey. His name hung on the air like a head of three flowers.

Divestiture was all of him now. Visible things could no longer hold their shape; the housing blocks looming over him meta-morphosed, became a dank cliff he must ascend.

Very slowly, he made his way to the stairwell. Darkness all around: the halogen wall lights smashed, the overhead defunct, the walls moist. Another world: a cavernous ante-chamber. He called the lift, waited what seemed an eternity. A tall Somali stepped out. There was some ancestral scorn on his face, some contempt of hunger, thirst and distance. He stared right through Farissey, passed on.

Farissey listened outside Jess's flat. No sound whatever. He unlocked the door, eased it open. A man was sitting in a chair placed directly in front of the high window. Farissey could see only his head, close-cropped. The head didn't stir. Nothing in the bathroom or bedroom. Nothing else in the front room but some sweaty stench, a stench he could taste. He tiptoed out, closed the door, left the Chubb key dangling from its lock.

He tried two flats without getting an answer. The third was answered by an elderly Somali woman. She stood proud-backed – no fear or even curiosity in her eyes. She spoke no English. He raised a fist to his ear, mimed the gesture of phoning; she drew him into the front room, bare but for a table, a little crockery, firewood stacked against the walls. Fumblingly, he found his address book in the inside pocket of his jacket, phoned Loudon Hargest.

On the way out, Farissey placed two pound coins on the table. The Somali woman blocked his access to the door. He offered her £5. She hissed at it, let the note flutter to the floor. Farissey picked up the note and retrieved the coins from the table.

Twenty minutes later, Hargest arrived bearing a large brief-case. He was wearing a rugby shirt and brown corduroys. He was quiet, his manner subdued, even evasive.

Farissey leaned back against the corridor wall. He returned Hargest's solemn stare. Something in his eyes that wouldn't announce itself.

Inside the flat, Hargest moved quickly, light-footed for a man of his size. He handcuffed Jess's left wrist to the arms of the heavy chair, strapped his ankles to its legs.

Farissey stationed himself between the chair and the window. Naked but for a towel around his midriff, Jess was still asleep in the chair. With thumb and index finger, Hargest did something to the back of Jess's neck. Jess shot bolt awake. Then he slumped back in the chair.

'Jack?' Jess said, a crudity in his features without those softening blond locks. His hair had been cropped to its brown roots. Pupils without their contact lenses; pupils like copper tacks squinted back.

Jess looked plumbeous, washed up but still agitated, like a gutted fish whose heart still continues to beat on a rock. His expression was utterly empty, like that of one who had looked too long, too deeply at some wound or genetic catastrophe properly hidden from mankind and from whose image a man can only return aghast, his wits blasted away, his mind like scorched earth.

'Jack?' Jess went to speak but instead his free hand fetched out as if to catch a bug or flea.

'I haven't got a bad effort in me,' Jess said, opening his empty palm as if by way of confirmation. 'Of all people, you should know that by now.' Jess closed his eyes, muttered to himself. Five minutes later, forensics arrived. Hargest took them to the window, pointed them to a run of fifteen wheelie bins in the courtyard. Five long minutes later and forensics had fished something substantial out of the bins, placed it in a plastic bag.

'Jack?' Jess called. But Farissey had already taken himself behind the chair.

'Jack!' Farissey heard Jess say as he joined the three police officers who stood silently – straight-backed and cartoonish – in the middle of the room.

'Jack?' But what Jess would see now was Loudon Hargest, his back to the window, sweaty and immovable, like a mountainous spectre against the fulgent midday light.

At the Central Police Station, Jess told Loudon Hargest everything he needed to hear. Jess spoke turbulently, layering detail over detail. He owned up to the murder of Christina Villers. He then spent more than an hour describing his movements since Saturday morning. Farissey sat on a chair in a corner of the interviewing room. Semi-delirious, he listened, felt frail energies flow in and out of himself in a circuit without waste or expenditure.

For the rest of his days, he would shape and replay Jess's deranged narrative. A word would haunt him. He remembered it from his study of anatomy. Exuviation: the shedding of skins.

Chapter Fifteen

The chair opposite had been empty when Jess awoke in the back room of Sven Books.

'One night – that was the deal,' Jimmy the Hat had said. 'Shop opens in an hour.'

Jess had rustled around in his holdall, noticed that a diary and a tape were missing. He'd shrugged, then smiled. 'That's all right, Jimmy. Thanks again.'

Then he'd walked the two miles to City Road, a grisly stretch of used-car salerooms, printing shops and takeaways. Through his eyes, that Saturday morning looked grainy, telescoped. Malevolence hung around the mists. He saw the world refracted at a distance. He tried to view the world as it would be without him. Shops, cars, grey, towering office buildings; all unwitnessed granite, grass, weeds, growth and decline.

Jess fell asleep in the barber's chair. He awoke to hear scissors clicking like crickets about a tent. In the mirror, he saw the florid barber at work, his toad-like eyes alert behind large-rimmed spectacles. Below, blond locks massed around his feet. 'A hard day's night,' Jess said, with some sickly attempt at a smile.

Back on City Road, he felt airy, relieved of the weight and

fuss of hair. He pulled the smart gaberdine mackintosh close to his body, buttoned it to cover his Mexican wedding shirt. He might almost look a paratrooper now, with his thick-set frame, his ever-alert eyes, his holdall. He could feel suspicious eyes peering into the back of his head as he crossed the road in the direction of the hardware store.

He had to push past a bus queue of old men and women, shrivelled, inert yet imploring in their light coats. He nodded politely, took all his cues from the energies building inside.

'Morning, sir. I need some knives for a restaurant kitchen,' Jess says, leaning on the counter, his lidless eyes half-focused on a Pirelli calendar.

Jess takes against the fat, balding Italian guy behind the counter: an Uncle Mario type – street angel/house devil.

'What sort of knives do you have in mind, sir?'

'Big knives, meat knives, carving knives,' Jess stutters, realising that he hasn't mapped this out at all.

Jess picks three knives at random from a catalogue.

'Your own restaurant?' the Italian asks on his return from the back room. He lays out three knives for inspection. People are behind Jess now. Not speaking to each other so much as squawking. Who were they? Why hadn't he seen them coming?

'Nah, my brother's – doing him a favour.'

'Local restaurant?'

'No – a way away, Canton.'

'These knives, they'll need sharpening if they're going to do a good job: making steak cuts, getting the meat from a neck.'

Jess begins to feel faint. *This guy has made me* – 'cuts', 'meat from a *neck*', 'a good *job*' – what with him having only the one job in mind. He stared blankly. The Italian guy suddenly looks bigger, wiser, menacing.

'Sharpeners, sir. In the kitchen.'

In the kitchen. In Jess's fantasy it took place in the kitchen. *The guy has read me. One telephone call and it'll never come off.*

'Sharpeners, in the kitchen?' Jess asks unsteadily.

'Your brother's restaurant, remember? Sharpeners in the kitchen.'

The Italian regards him for an instant before breaking into a bearish smile.

'Some wicked black going around at the moment.'

Jess smiles himself. *He's got me down as a stonehead and no more.*

'Sure, sure,' Jess says, paying for the knives as they're being sharpened. 'Wicked's the word, man.'

He walked back into town, the knives chinking in his holdall. At the open-air café on the Hayes Island, he ordered an all-day breakfast. The food and tea arrived at the table with a clatter. Jess recoiled from the eggs, prodded them for creatural signs. A phrase popped into his mind: poached eyes on ghost. He ate the toast only, drank his tea and left in the direction of Canton. He'd walked some twenty yards when he looked back to see scores of pigeons attacking the plate like some gigantic feathery organism in peristalsis. It made him think of life, teeming life, the throbbing sickness he felt all around him. Later that day, Jess fancied that the breakfast, his queasy stomach, the café were all there just to lure that image into its being.

He called in at his mother's flat in Canton. His mother was a slim, hyperactive woman in her late fifties. She opened the door wearing jeans and a psychedelic blouse. She tried to look cheerful but strain showed around her mouth. 'All those lovely blond locks, all nothing now.' She ran her hands across his head, some pleading in her eyes. He followed her into the front room.

'And what about this mess you're in?' she asked, her arthritic hands folded into her lap like a tangle of drowned roots. The Baja brothers had called round. They'd menaced her, taken away one of Jess's guitars; in part-repayment, so they said.

'It was a one-off,' he said with a perfunctory air. He looked at the large fish tank in the corner of the room, the fish busying around like so many hapless impressions that had yet to become ideas.

'Well, get yourself sorted out, for crying out loud! And when am I going to meet this Victoria? She's making me a grandmother and instead of setting up with her – well, you're spending most of your time here.'

'You'll see her soon enough. Talking of which, I need some money for baby things.'

She didn't reply. Silently, she cooked a pasta dinner, enlivened by the basil she grew at the kitchen window. His sister joined them. She was wearing a threadbare tracksuit, a white flower tied into her tangled, lifeless hair.

After dinner the three smoked a few joints of sickly sweet home-grown. They smoked silently, a steady breeze of disappointment emanating from the mother. 'Both of you back with me all these years later,' she said breathily. 'It's all upside down.'

'What you doing tonight?' his sister asked.

'Going down the docks,' he replied without looking up. His sister phoned a friend, went upstairs to wash and change.

He packed a washbag upstairs, soaked his feet in a bucket. He called his sister into the bedroom. He lay back on the bed, cradled his head as she cut his toenails. He couldn't mutilate himself. He lay in peace, puzzling over the legend of how nails are dead on the body yet live after the body.

Downstairs, his mother squeezed £100 into his hand. Her careworn look told him that this was the last time, the last chance. His sister came down in a black blouse and denim skirt, strutted through the front door without a word for the mother.

On the way through Grangetown he bought a bottle of Baileys. 'We used to like this when we were kids,' he said. They passed it back and forth as they walked. Every so often they had to stop. She had bad cramps with her period. They sat at the iron bridge between Grangetown and the docks. Autumnal shadows threshed about the windy bay.

'You know what helps cramps,' he said.

She stared without response at the River Taff below. There was nothing of perturbation or compliance in her eyes. He tried to recall the Hindu myth about menstruation. A fish swims from a shoreless expanse into time. It enters time through the gullet of a woman, swims down those sweeping rivers, becomes incarnate in the menstrual fluid, finds its way into the oceans. *Blood sliding through her like a fish; icy cramps.*

They moved around Butetown bars in search of the quarter of hash she wanted. 'Feels like running, this,' she said, as they sat side by side drinking cider in the White Hart.

'Fugitives,' he said. 'Like when Mum managed the aquarium.' He looked down at her short denim skirt. Her unstockinged legs looked like so much crumpled blubber to him.

Come midnight, she headed off to the North Star. Jess went to the Casablanca. He felt cool, frightening, eyes on him as he paid his £3 at the door. Some ragga Jess didn't recognise thumped on in the gloom and sanctity of this nightclub. He looked around for some piece of well-used trash he'd flatter, empathise with and pick up for the night's bed. Not seeing any of the girls, he headed straight for the score.

The Inited Idren were lined up in the corridor leading to the lavatories. They were touting £10 hash and grass deals. The Idren eyed Jess wryly and with sinister smiles. They were stoned, immobile, ever-watchful like warriors.

'Carl wants to see you,' Primo said, passing across a bag of sulphate for inspection. 'He's already seen your spar, Farissey. Seen *to* him . . . You get me?'

Jess felt tears rise, fought them back. 'Tell Carl I want to square things. Make us both a bit of money. Bring down a shipping order of E from Manchester.'

Jess dusted a finger and licked the sulphate. Might be a bit underweight, but the quality was passable. No ephedrine in the mix; he couldn't taste any other cut. Jess looked into the polythene speed bag; summoned seriousness from his stomach like a diver at a cliff-face.

'Let me hoover the whole deal off your hand. I don't want to walk out of here carrying.'

'The whole deal! Spar, you're fucking around. This is two grammes of good whiz you're doing here. Trying to set an Olympic record or something?'

Jess put £40 into Primo's hand.

'You're just like a Brazilian footballer, Primo . . . Pele, Zico, Socrates – one name's enough.'

'Yeah, man. One name's enough where the cops are concerned. You ready now?'

Jess would be ready. He would be of one vision. He'd never sleep again. Those few days and nights and dawns could roll into one another in the savage series he'd mapped.

The club seemed to come to a standstill as he whisked through the dancers and bouncers to the crisp and chastening night, not knowing if it was the world that ground to a halt or if he had suddenly overreached it, wound as he was beyond compass or vigil, his mind motoring like a spinning top through empty squares.

At two o'clock he rejoined his sister at the North Star. She was way, way stoned with barbs: incomprehensible, almost.

'Ya back. What's happening?' she asked, almost slobbering.

He looked at the curled-up auburn hair, her puffed-up face, those watery, senseless eyes, their lids like pointed hoods.

'We'll go back to Atlantic Wharf. There's still some bedding there.'

She got to her feet, took to the floor, not so much to dance as to crash and stumble to some dreary soul track. He took her out of the club, shouldered her to the bare flat. She crashed out in her clothes on a mattress in the front room. Her contact lenses were still in. They merged with the film of her porcine eyes. Running a hand over her sleeping head, he looked at the bureau. Holy oils, he thought. I could anoint her. Now she's safe.

There would never be urgency like it again. He paced around her prone body. He thought of the half-lights of the Butetown Aquarium; eerie lights, refracted through water. Then that thing invaded her: a monstrosity; a stupid-mouthed fish; nothing to do with him.

Soon after the abortion, his father disappeared into the wilderness of South London. Suspected something, most like. Picked up some word in Newport. Late one night, downstairs in the aquarium, his mother explained how things go wrong between men and women and how it's the woman the man leaves, never his children. Jess listened like a child who can understand departure in the active case of 'I kill you' but not the remote, causeless cases of death or abandonment.

He recalls heading for the door of the aquarium and running and running and running, how far he couldn't know. He ended up outside the docks, somewhere on Rover Way, beside the gypsy caravans with a dog barking in the distance, the sky as dark as coal, and him thinking that he could triumph over loss and absence, above all that, as he was, in the muted eternity of his grief and rage.

He got back into school, but never made up the lost time. He worked out, built muscle, brought on his guitar playing. He picked up girls in droves, discarded them, won the respect of his peers and put grave, sadistic distance between himself and women, all women. And it worked well enough until Farissey went away to study pharmacy. He mimicked Farissey even then, went away himself. He played guitar in Amsterdam bands, learned a higher-class drug culture. It all landed up with him working in an onion-pickling factory. But back in Cardiff, he was one step ahead. He could hold his own in Butetown thereafter.

'Like you will now,' he said to himself in the bathroom mirror. He flushed his contact lenses down the lavatory. Six a.m. his watch said. He looked at it with disbelief. He didn't realise that he'd paced every inch of this gutted flat. Nor that he'd been jabbering to himself for hours and hours, hand-rolling cigarette after cigarette.

'When's the day?' he asked himself at the mirror. Without lenses, his eyes now had a cruel and plummetless quality: a surface hardness and a glint like steel.

'Yesterday! You did just great. Like a schoolkid – you already passed that exam.'

'How did I do it?'

'From the outside in, then the inside out. Excavated. Evacuated.'

Look at that cunt, he thought as he shaved. Look at him. In a mirror's dawn and lacerations and light. Ready for shaving and pulling faces, grimacing. Like his face was the only fucking face in the world.

'Get the fuck out of my face.'

'You're stuck, trapped in my gaze. Everywhere.'

'You don't fuck with me.'

'You don't fuck.'

The window was bright with the clear, sharp, piercing violence of that autumn's sun. It would be one of a series of sleepless dawns and jangling, dehydrated mornings. He chewed his tongue until it bled; wishing for curtains, veils and unveiling. *Unmasking*: as though he could slice clean that thin skin strapped over his face.

'Know me for what I am, for what I'm worth,' he repeated over and over.

Scalding, dry ice, muscles excoriate, all the organs overwrought against sleep; slow, clear, bodywarm-water dribbling into his trousers.

He doesn't know how long he'd been at the mirror. He shrieked when he saw blood in the sink. There wasn't a rag in the flat. Panicked, he found a tampon in his sister's handbag and ran it under cold water. He applied it below his Adam's apple, stanched the shaving wound.

His sister stirred as he dressed. She crawled into the bathroom. He heard her vomit; vomit over and over. Then he heard her sobbing.

'Go back to sleep,' he said at the door.

'I'm going back to Canton,' she said. 'I can't stay in these clothes.'

Vomit on her blouse and skirt. 'That'll wash out in the bath here.'

'No,' she said, getting to her feet. She used a towel rail for support. She pointed at his knee-length green mackintosh, the yellow scarf flung raffishly over one shoulder, the holdall over another. 'Where you going, anyway?'

'To straighten things out.'

She sat down on the edge of the bath, another wave of nausea on her, put her head in her hands. 'Should straighten yourself out first,' she said.

It was 9.30 that Sunday morning when Jess reached the pharmacy. Victoria answered the door in a purple bathrobe, her hair, thick with henna, brushed back. It took her a few seconds to recognise him.

'Where's Jack?' She was shivering slightly.

'I'm not going to talk out here,' he replied. His voice was dry, raspy. He followed her upstairs and into the kitchen. There was nothing between them, no energy in his field now Farissey was gone. He looked down at the cigarette he was rolling. There were tears in his eyes. He felt wrecked, abraded, eaten away on the inside and outside. Everything but the expensive mackintosh was in stained disarray. How far from that image he projected. A precise man who showered incessantly, ironed with absolute precision, applied deodorant, aftershave, lotions on a twice-daily basis.

Jess leaned on the kitchen door, placed the holdall at his feet. He watched as she went to the sink, carried on washing henna through her hair. Jess joined the tips of his fingers together, felt a sharp charge coursing through his nerves. 'The Bajas got to Jack.'

'I could have worked that out myself,' she said.

'It's all about him – at the end of the day. You know that, don't you?' he shouted after her as she went into a bedroom.

She came back with a hairdryer and brush.

'If something really bad's happened to Jack,' she said, her words measured but shaky, exasperation in her tone. 'Say he doesn't come back. You know what would happen to you, don't you?'

'What?'

'You'd look in the mirror and it'd be empty.'

'Dead smart, dead fucking smart. Soon as I get a bit of business done, I'm going to look after him, make him whole again.'

'What bit of business?' There was real disdain in her now; reckless disdain.

'Sort things out between us and Carl Baja.'

'*You* sort Carl Baja out?'

She put down the hairdryer without turning it off. 'Look, Jess,' she said, calmly now. 'If you know where Jack is, tell me. I've rung all the hospitals. If you don't know, leave me alone.' She spoke slowly, as if to a child or refugee. He felt the anger mount in him like another drug. 'If this is about the baby,' she continued, 'well, forget it. We've decided.'

'The baby,' he said. 'The fucking baby.' His voice fell off with tired superiority. 'I had the Idren round my house, threatening my mother. I can't move without looking over my fucking shoulder. You set things up so they could get their hands on those documents. What about that? What about—?'

'It was an accident.' She went back to drying and brushing her hair. He paced across the kitchen, pulled a gin bottle from the cupboard. He unscrewed the top and took a hefty draught.

'Don't worry, Jack bought it,' she said sardonically.

'I'm not worried,' he said. He raised the gin bottle to his lips, twisted towards her in mid-gulp.

In that instant she would have seen him, fully six foot tall ravaged, wild, defining the kitchen doorway, which would be her last prospect, blackened around the cheekbones, a heavy alcohol flush over ashen skin, pinpricks for eyes, visionless, fixed, an uncanny breeze within him and in his wake. She would have known there wasn't anything behind her but a dresser, pots and pans, the rough, bumped wall, the old black range. But nothing happened just then and he stayed grinning at her: foul-toothed and cherubic in a mixture of superior malice and innocence hurt and recaptured from its blights – grin of a boy unburied, a child revenant at the railings and reborn into its dusk games.

He placed the holdall at his feet in the little eternity in

which she watches and holds herself upright, brushes her hair mechanically – as though she was smacked up or in the grip of some autism – and feigns unconcern, incuriosity.

'Jess, you don't want anything to do with this baby. That suits me down to the ground,' she said. There was a warble in her voice: a welcome detail, one he couldn't have foreseen, until he knew, until *now*.

'Down to the ground?' he repeated, a slight sneer in his tone.

All electric and sort of velvet. No way he could leave the kitchen. After all, the fat Uncle Mario in the shop had seen it all coming. It was preordained: it just *had* to be this way.

'C'mon. Say something that means something. Anything. Say something about those fucking documents. The Idren after me. Say something about that. Say something about what they might have done to Jack. C'mon. Say.'

His face was curled up with fury; ugly, very ugly, like his wagging finger, that beak-like, predatory nose, placed on his face like bright warning colours on an exotic beetle. She was running scared, shaking and stock-still all in an instant.

'Say what, Jess?' Something rustled in her voice, like wind through leaves. Power and light and untroubled azure and baptising clouds, he felt.

'Uh . . .' He let it run, throaty and baritone, as long as his voice might hold, and as long as he could feel that it wouldn't be him who'd be talking, that something else was calling him, choosing him as a channel; as long as he knew that he was his own child, father to himself, that he'd birthed something else into his being. Some other speech, fire forming and unfurling, and phoenix wings in his skull, like he might fly or fall into cinder, into pieces and burial earth.

'This time. This time. And no fucking around. Right here; any minute now.'

His scarf must have slipped from his shoulder because he catches something at the edges of his vision and he thinks there's something going for him, for his throat, and he spins around and kicks the holdall he's laid by the kitchen table and Victoria hears a chink altogether graver than the bright chime of bottles.

That was the only chance she'd had as he realises that her chances are his chances too. He thinks the slipping scarf is a snake or a lizard flashing out its tongue over his shoulder, like the kitchen carpet might nurture, red and crass and reptilian as it was. Everything so cold; him, her, the carpet, the range, the table, the electric light, the tap still running.

'You don't fuck with me,' he says, resuming his stand before her, remote as she looks now, as though a mist had blown into the kitchen; Victoria, pent with fear, her back to the range. 'Not any more,' he adds, realising that he's got her now. She'll never move of her own free will again.

'You don't fuck. You don't fuck with me.'

He's walking towards her. Putting one foot in front of another with the deliberation of a cripple or skyline walker. He takes her face in his hands and twists it. Like he wants to twist her head clean off her shoulders. He smashes her head off the edge of the range. Blood, so much blood, in a moment otherwise frozen.

Perhaps she's not too badly hurt because she's mewling now and pleading, some shit like 'Jess, Jess. Why? For God's sake, why?' He head-butts her three or four times and she's really out of it now, and he plunges her head into the sink, into foul greenish water slick with shampoo foam, and holds her there until he can hear her gurgling and her breath pushing up and out with the bubbles. The water looks like it's got eyes in it, baby eyes, no, still-forming yolky eyes. That's when the knives occur to him, and he pulls one out with his free hand and she seems to know what's happening because she screams 'Jess, for God's sake. It's your baby, I know it's yours', and he tells her to shut the fuck up as he holds one knife to her and scrambles around with his free hand for another.

Why did he think to buy so many knives? When he knew they'd be too many? That's what he had to ask as he spreads her buttocks just before he starts stabbing. Her bathrobe gets all mixed up with the blood and he knows the knife is his tongue and he's making the kind of love he's always wanted to make; but none of it is coming out clean – it's coming out in broken waters and blood and mush, nothing to squeeze in the palm of his hand, nothing to squeeze the life and warmth out of, and all he wanted was one lump of meat to have broiling in there, hot and stewing and rare, so rare, but it's no more solid than maggots and he just flails and stabs, triumphant and absent, upright, fixed, rigid, while she drops like another leaf from the season's trees.

No, no: it's slow, heavy, slumping, and it's something else that's light and leaving, like life from bodies as we rise, up, up, through purples and indigos, vermilion and blue, seeking the perfect, permanent transparence, and it's just gone like air from a balloon, leaving only wrinkles and withers behind, lifeless, limp, rags when the doll's been ripped from the stitching. Bitch and dog-whore, cosseted by her sex and her condition from the violences, now safe, secure, immune again and it only being an instant when he'd taken her to this place, shown her how it'd been for him and then she was OK, bitch that had repudiated him again and when most he needed her, when most he needed Farissey. And Jess himself? Looking down, drugged, unreflected, hollowed, without energy to shift his gaze, all the still-swirling speed mixing with the adrenalin to hold him in a bodiless trembling: a still of fate and incomprehension; proud, laughable, like a monster of destiny and cartoon.

Her blood. Some of his? Hers on his hands, his clothes. And that shallow viscous swamp he's standing in. He hears the steady yet hurried sound of a hairdryer. If only he could talk to Jack Farissey. If only that adolescent pact still held. They'd sworn so often on those faraway winter evenings to be brothers; no matter what happened, however bad, however bloody. Talk about what? About Victoria? Why, she didn't exist now any more than he did.

Chapter Sixteen

Sleepless, he lived the succeeding days in a waking dream. He moved between glazed indifference and moments of agonised lucidity. An afternoon would vanish in a blink. Five minutes at a counter would wear away like coastal rock.

Sleepless, he feared she might haunt his dreams. One afternoon, dozing, he dreamed she walked across the bay in gilt and glided air, leaving behind a train of auras, a special resonance that only deep loneliness can confer on others, on films, on paintings, on memories. Another time, she opened a cloak to reveal a torso composed of a thousand stitches.

He heard her voice in the rudder of a ship, an ambulance siren, in the silence of sullen, after-dark quays. He half-expected to meet her on his wanderings just as the recently bereaved would not find it unnatural to see the chair opposite full once again with a mirthful or cajoling spouse, or to feel a hand fold itself into theirs on a country lane or riverside walk. In all this, he was not disposed to forget the hell that they'd lived through, only to recall it as a hell less horrible than now.

On Wednesday afternoon he walked Butetown with no aim beyond finding a shard or echo of himself in the sheltering

buildings and alleyways of his youth. As he walked, he saw
the changes made by the Docklands Regeneration Corporation.
How much swifter the face of a city changes than the people it
shelters. He remembered hearing of a nomadic tribe who'd rest
every three days to let their souls catch up. No such sense was
shown in cities.

At Pier Head he lit a cigarette, looked over the estuary water.
It was neither his water any more nor the prospect that had
whispered adventure to the lonely yearnings of his youth. It was
flat but alive with wagtails and mandarin ducks. He huddled
against the windy bay and its strange sun, burstling in flints
today, all magnesium and judgement. He could laugh and did,
and the still water returned his laughter. He thought he heard
the name echo in the hollow of the wind. 'Jack. Jack Farissey.'
Why hadn't anyone come for him? Why had he of all people
been called on to survive, he who would have changed places
with any of them? Had everything in his existence shored up
towards this absence? He tried to think it through, but was
again beyond caring, beyond asking, beyond wondering, as he
wandered the wide spaces, waiting his turn.

Just after dawn the next day, he packed a bag and walked to
the railway station. Under the Bute Street Bridge, a whistling
dosser woman wheeled a supermarket trolley brimful with damp
newspapers and empty food cartons.

His body began to feel heavy with him: steps leaden and
indecipherable. He attempted to stroll but once more fell into
the footsteps of the dead. He imagined that the city was a citadel
on a page of sea; the body, a corporeal envelope addressed to
God. On Caroline Street, he felt the wind gather up newspapers
and chip wrappers in one great litter. He rejected this image
because of its very spontaneity.

At the station, he stood on the platform as the Paddington
train pulled in and pulled out. He wondered how things would
have gone if Christina had just stayed on the train: serene,
smoking a cigarette, gazing at a single-track line and a small

approaching bridge, letting the pylons, enclosures, tracks, the countryside, the sidings and bridges all vanish behind her.

He decided against any train, picked up a station taxi. He lit a cigarette, flicked his ash out of the window. Two cigarettes later, the taxi rose beyond Cardiff's city limits.

The taxi pulled up in front of reception in the holiday camp. He noted the scatter of lifeless trees, the grey forecourt, the neat rectangles of grass. In the distance, morning sun bounced off a Perspex roof.

The fare was £25. In his distraction, he handed over £40. He left the remainder as a tip, brushed aside the cabby's gratitude.

A washed-out, listless redcoat emerged from the revolving door. It was the last week of the season, the redcoat explained. No more than fifty of the fourteen hundred chalets were occupied.

His chalet consisted of an iron bed, a small bedside table, a phone with no outside line, a shower and sink on which sat a detergent-stained glass. There was also a radio, a map of the camp, a guide to entertainments. His view looked on to a series of park rides that were partially covered by a tarpaulin. Opposite was a bingo hall and a grill-restaurant. He soaked up the details with bleak satisfaction.

Alone, he pulled three bottles of Scotch from his holdall. He lay on the bed, sipped from the first. That afternoon he played pinball with moronic concentration, forcing the machine to concede twelve replays. He then played three frames of solitary snooker and retired to a dead bar. The bartender had a freckled face, sandy hair waved up into a floppy middle parting. He enthused about one-night stands being a perk of a redcoat's job. His left cheek twitched as he spoke.

Come dusk, he picked at steak and chips in the grill-restaurant. An elderly man on a nearby table was smoking the unusual pipe tobacco his father had favoured. The pedestrian coincidence led him into a claustrophobic conversation with the man's wife.

After dinner, he drank whisky outside his chalet. He listened politely as a middle-aged woman complained of her husband's gambling, of how he'd sold family heirlooms for a song. Her arms were flabby, bulged from the sleeves of a floral dress. She had an arthritic labrador in tow. He stroked the dog, sipped whisky from the clouded glass. The taste of the whisky, the acrid kick of the tobacco, a sharp breeze on his face – all seemed just worth the effort of living.

Later, he walked to the fence beyond which was a busy A-road. He sat on a bench, watched the corpuscular stream of cars. He envied their sense of destination, resolved to become one with this steady, arterial pulse.

That night in the bar, he sat opposite a tastefully dressed woman of about forty. He observed her discreetly, curious as to why such a woman would holiday in such a place. She wore a Hermès silk scarf, a jewelled brooch attached to a dress of thankless beige. She was fine-boned and angular, a face sculpted securely by careful auburn curls. There was nothing harsh in her; even the worry in her eyes was gentle, compassionate and without rebuke. Something in her, too, that he wanted, but couldn't quite comprehend. Some peace, some grace recalled to him, just as certain mauve evenings, faces across a hallway, abandoned buildings or half-heard pianos can intimate a precious mood now lost.

'Are you from around here?' she asked in a soft Welsh accent. Her manner was cool but ironic, as though it might break into mirth or intimacy.

'Cardiff. The docks.'

'What we used to call Tiger Bay?'

'Yeah, but it isn't like that any more.'

'Don't I know it.' She went on to explain that she was using the holiday camp as a base from which to make daily visits to Cardiff, often returning as late as 10 p.m. 'It's strange,' she said, 'but I can't stay there overnight. Too many memories? I don't know.'

Over a few drinks, he learned that her name was Susan. As a teenager she'd moved from the Valleys to Cardiff, made a disastrous marriage. A child followed but didn't stop her taking off with a Swansea businessman. Yes, she'd lost her Valleys accent, but it was expected of her that she renounce her roots. Technically, her second marriage had been bigamous, but her Cardiff husband was too much of a drunk and a nobody to know, still less care.

'I had to leave a tiny little daughter behind me,' she said. 'I left her once and she left me for good.' She paused, her attention taken by two girls entering the bar; gaudy in dress but with a sleekness in their beings. Escorts, he surmised; one with her hip cocked out, all invite and defiance; the other with a hard, survivalistic sneer around her mouth. Susan soaked it all up; those gentle, inquisitive eyes poised just this side of provocation.

'You must think this woman's crackers,' she said, 'that she doesn't know the score.'

'I was trying not to think anything.'

'Thank you. You're a gentleman. But don't worry – I've been doing this for some time.'

'Doing what?'

'Observing,' she said, with that mixture of mischief and sadness that so drew him.

Come eleven o'clock, he offered to walk her to her chalet.

'Thank you,' she said, offering her hand. 'But I'd rather have the pleasure of leaving you where I had the good fortune to find you.'

That night he dreamed copiously. First, of a misty and ethereal dawn through whose folds and flounces he descended, lightly, like a dove, the steps of a law court. He looked for Victoria only to be told that she had left him for a realm of ascending colours, each colour a chamber through which she glided to an impossible summit, always beyond, and into a viewless light where colour and nuance were no more. In a second, almost awake and commenting on the pageant, he was dying of lung cancer and she had appeared beside his bed. She beckoned. He smiled one of his rare, starry smiles, arose from his bed and followed. Both dreams were of Victoria; in each he was placid. A third, incorporating Christina but whose broad content he could not recall, told him that he'd conflated past and future, four figures and two bodies in a single theatre of sacrifice.

In a final dream, he was walking through Butetown with Susan. The Custom House was now a wilderness of mirrors. She took lessons from the hustlers about dress codes, struck poses. Her identity got lost in the reflections until her name became all names, her face all those faces he would never see again. Next, he was in a Cardiff hotel room with Susan restored to herself. He was afraid, but when she stripped to the waist he knew it was right that they should make love amid a bittersweet smell of flesh just leavening into middle age. He felt regret afterwards. It had been clumsy, slow and mournful. But somehow it had been purifying, too, as though they were sucking their sadnesses into each other, making them mean-ingful in that peculiar pathos only sympathetic strangers can generate, glad of the strangeness, secure in its soft and unde-manding arms. Then she began to weep in a series of stifled sobs, drawing her upset back into herself.

'I'm sorry,' she said. 'It's not you – it's my daughter.'

Awake, the words resounded in his mind. Was she making these daily trips to Cardiff as a sort of pilgrimage? Like soldiers who return to the place of a friend's death, not to some church-yard, trees and a stone?

Of all the sad quests, he thought. Cruising around in search of knowledge rather than excitement or distraction: looking at the girls, trying to discover the fears, depressions and confusions that had led them to this abandonment. Trying to understand why her daughter had chosen this deadly lifestyle. Too late, she had returned. A ghost in search of a ghost, guilt and incom-pletion drawing her back to atone, understand, to overlay the shadow of herself on the shadow of departure.

Cruel pre-dawn light filled the room as he opened the thin, yellow-sheened curtains. He showered, dressed, lay on the bed. His waking world seemed altogether less real than his dream life. Living in reality, he ventured, gave one little beyond more

of the real. He phoned reception. There was no woman registered with the name Susan, or anyone fitting her description.

He lay on the bed, cradled his head, became aware of each
moment dissolving into the past. Time pulsed away from his
blood. He disowned the past, not only its content but its
concept. The future stretched before him as a long, dank,
imageless tunnel starting here and ending nowhere.

He was in hiding, in flight from the police, from the Baja
brothers. Names, events and identities folded in and out of one
another like the figures of a fugue.

Perhaps no one was coming for him. In that case, he could
count the minutes, urge them to form hours and days, but there
would be no terminus. If no one was coming for him, then this
was waiting and world without end. Might the murder of Victoria have been a dream? The thought gave him no repose
because these succeeding days would also be a dream.

He lay drinking for two hours. He hid his whisky when the
cleaner knocked on the door. She looked around with downcast
eyes. Her hair was jet black, tied into a long, ragged ponytail. He
watched her scrubbing the floor, goat-like and silent. He looked
on with some respect and tenderness.

At 10.30 that morning he stepped outside. He stood in his
shadow. A little boy and girl squabbled over a stick of candyfloss.
The boy cried when floss got into his eyes.

He looked up at the sky. All the colours had recomposed. A
cloudless blue of the sky, the deep, dull green of bark on trees
beyond the camp, gold on dull green, the beige of a barn dedicated to five-a-side football, the mud-red of its roof. Nothing
jagged, sharp, pronounced, or anything mushed-up, indistinct,
hazy or confused, the day itself breezeless, all objects static or
travelling along their rightful paths; engines hissing, cars
running in airy currents on the perimeter road.

He smoked two cigarettes, back to back. The smoke mingled
with adrenalin and relief, ran deep into him. He felt as though
his lungs were inexhaustible caverns: grand, greedy, alive.

The idea came back to him as reality, then; the redeeming
idea, the one that came from some small, precarious, yet pre-

cious part of himself that knew everything to be wretched but not irrevocable and, like some savage illness, subject to the ordinance of time, of passing, of forgetting, of healing or death.

He turned on the radio, listened for the date. On that Wednesday, he was exactly seven weeks short of his thirty-ninth birthday. He drank three fingers of whisky from the cloudy glass, phoned the bar. It was eleven o'clock. With the promise of a good tip, the bartender agreed to bring across a cheese sandwich at two that afternoon.

He brushed his teeth assiduously, shaved. Where would he go? Over to some cold shore without song or undermusic? He dug around in his holdall. He washed down the seconal with whisky until he reached two hundred, stood with his face against the chalet wall. He closed his eyes, wondered why he had been called on to endure this dream. He saw the long, lustreless expanse that had been his school playground. He was just joining that expanse with a railing and a leafy lane when his body slumped.

Down on one knee, he had just enough mind to know that this would not be the watery grave of his imaginings, but death by default. He would be found out of season, crumpled, faithless and open-mouthed on a chalet floor of this colour-coded holiday camp.